Tea Shop Folly

Book One, The Christy Cousins Series

By

Carrie Fancett Pagels

Hearts Overcoming Press

Second Edition

July, 2016, first edition/
February 2017 second edition

ASIN-10
ISBN-13: 978-0-9971908-2-3
ISBN-10:0997190825

Cover by Roseanna White

Hearts Overcoming Press

Dedicated
To
Diana Lynn (Taylor) Flowers

An amazing reviewer, blogger, Beta reader,
and friend!

Prologue

Blue Ridge Mountains, 1895

Smoke clung to the treetops low in the valley while mist circled the craggy mountaintop cabin. Lilly trudged down to Whiskey Creek to bring up water, breathing a prayer, *Let Mama live.* At least she'd been able to get a fire going, to warm her mother. But daily chores waited on no one, certainly not for Lilly.

Daisy, her youngest sister, ran up alongside Lilly. "Why we gotta haul our water from the river?"

"The well went dry." The last of the money had run out, too. Lilly's hope was nearly exhausted.

A sunbeam cracked through the milky haze overhead and the two paused to look skyward.

"That's purty." Her tow-headed sister wiped her eyes with her free hand. "Wish Mama could come out to see it."

Lilly blinked back her own tears. "She's gonna get through this, don't you worry."

"How?" Her sister's husky voice tore through the last of Lilly's thin defenses. She dropped her buckets and pulled the twelve-year-old close to her side.

"I don't know, but God does." Her words rang hollow, though. Mama was dying, there was little left to feed the girls.

Daisy sniffed. "He sure ain't showing it."

"Sometimes He takes His time to help us. . ." Help them what? Grow in faith? In trust?

"We sure could use some help."

Lilly's knees suddenly throbbed. She'd spent so much time on them, in prayer, that she almost expected to see callouses appear on them. She exhaled loudly and released Daisy. "For now, He gave Mama five strong daughters to take care of her – and each other."

"And cousin Eb, don't forget him."

It had been a week since their strapping Christy cousin had visited, promising to return with help from their aunt and uncle. But the only thing she'd seen from Eb had been his ability to consume vast amounts of their food in a short time. Truth be told, she'd been relieved when he'd left them.

She handed Daisy one of her buckets. "Let's get going – this pail isn't gonna collect water by itself."

Soon, they'd returned with the filled pails. They poured the water into a kettle over an outdoor fire, to make the water safer for drinking. Now it would have to cool.

"Get me the tea kettle, Daisy, and we'll steep some sassafras tea for Mama and the girls." Lilly swiped a hand across her forehead.

"Ho to the house!" Eb's deep voice carried up from the path.

Lilly cringed. *Lord, please let him be a help and not a hindrance.*

Daisy ran off to meet their burly dark-haired cousin, apparently forgetting all about the tea kettle.

When he rounded the corner, with an overflowing crate of sacks of food, Lilly flushed in shame at her earlier thoughts. "Thank you, Eb!"

He set the crates down on the ground with a grunt.

Daisy clapped her hands and plucked out a tin of real tea. "I'll get the kettle now and tell Mama!"

Lines around Eb's dark eyes crinkled as he grinned. "I got a letter for ya, too."

"Oh?" The only letters they'd received recently had been from unpaid accounts in town.

"Aunt Lillian done passed away."

"Oh! I'm so sorry to hear that!" Her Aunt Lill, for whom she'd been named, lived far in the north of Michigan, even farther up than her lumberjack cousins.

"Got something for you from her lawyer."

Lilly froze. Lawyers meant bad news. What now?

Eb drew closer. "No need to frown."

She squinted at him. "Why not?"

A blush crept up his neck as he passed her a large brown envelope that had been unsealed. "I didn't open it – Pa did. He said ya got a train ticket in there and a check and I'm to cash that check right away for the family and that he can't keep providing for ya." He sucked in a deep breath.

Lilly sank onto a tree stump they used as an outdoor seat. Whether her uncle meant he'd not help the family or not Lilly, she wasn't sure. On his last visit, Eb informed her that his father felt that an "old maid like you shoulda married Clyde when he asked and helped her family." She cringed at the thought of ever marrying the man she suspected of killing her father.

She lifted the flap and opened the letter and scanned it. *Lillian Smith, heir and executor.* Her heart hitched up into her throat. "I know what an heir is but not an executor."

Eb shrugged. "I reckon yer about to find out."

Chapter 1

Sault Ste. Marie, Michigan

Stale odors of pipe smoke mingled with aging leather and dried flowers in dire need of replacing at the elderly attorney's office. Lilly's stomach growled. The check that had been sent for her travel expenses had gone toward buying food for her siblings and to pay for a physician for her mother. The slim balance that remained had made the past two days almost unbearable with hunger.

She tapped her scuffed boot toes impatiently and glanced around the room. The uncomfortable chair with ornate carvings dug through the thin cotton of her jacket.

Two matrons knit by the large windows that fronted the building. One shifted to the edge of her chair. "Why a wealthy attorney like Mr. Baisley would keep these horrid Eastlake chairs in his office, I do not know."

The thin white-haired woman sitting next to her nodded, not pausing at all in the clicking of her needles together. She looked over at Lilly. Instead of the disapproval Lilly expected, because of her ragged clothing, the woman smiled at her.

Lilly grinned back, then averted her eyes feeling like a naughty child for smiling when she should be sitting here mourning her aunt's loss while awaiting the executor's instructions. Dressed as she was, in Mama's faded calico church dress, she didn't even have proper mourning clothes. It was hard to think of anything but getting something into her stomach as soon as she could.

The door to the office creaked open and a thin, bent man crooked a finger at her. "Miss Smith? I'm Mr. Baisley. Come this way."

Clutching her carpetbag to her chest, Lilly rose and followed him into his office. He motioned to a straight-back padded seat chair, while he made his way, with slow effort, around his large black desk. With the only light in the room coming from the windows behind him and two gaslights on opposite walls, Lilly couldn't quite make out all the engravings in the hideous piece of furniture.

"Sit down, miss, eh?"

The crispness of the man's northern Michigan accent caused her to flinch. "Yes, sir."

"Your aunt Lillian was a wonderful woman. A bit eccentric with all those fripperies, but a godly lady nonetheless."

"Yes, sir." Was that the right thing to say?

What little Lilly had known of her great Aunt, for whom she'd been named, was that she'd lived a hard life. She and her husband had lost their Virginia home during the war. Then Uncle Oscar had died in an accident in the Soo Locks. Her two sons went down on the same ship in a Lake Superior squall. And Aunt Lillian's daughter passed away during a difficult childbirth. For the past decade, Auntie had resided alone, often sending them picture postal cards of the area. She was active in her church and drew comfort from her faith, often participating in fundraisers. While Mama would never have let her aunt know how difficult things were, she thought Aunt Lillian suspected.

"Miss, did you hear what I said?" The lawyer peered over his round spectacles at her.

"No, sir." She clasped her chapped hands together, over her growling stomach.

"You're the sole heir and all of the estate reverts to you immediately."

That was what Mama had said might happen, but it didn't seem possible. Lilly's head swam and she grabbed the chair's arms.

"As her attorney, I'll offer you guidance, and she's even provided for that expense in advance."

Lilly nodded. She blinked as her heart rate sped up. It was true. "What...what do I do next?" Besides filling her belly?

Mr. Baisley opened a legal envelope and handed her a list and several keys. "Let's go over this one item at a time."

The noise of construction still grated on Theo even these many months since he'd arrived in Sault Sainte Marie from Detroit. Some engineer he was – he couldn't even manage the waterfront's stressors despite training for years and having worked at shipyards from Newport News, Virginia, to Boston, Massachusetts. What he needed was a good strong cup of English tea – like his grandmother used to make, God rest her soul.

"Theodore! Come look at this latest correction in the design." His superior, Franz Sehler, a broad-shouldered German engineer in his fifties, jabbed a finger at the blueprints on his littered desk. Dirty coffee cups, wads of crushed paper, and broken pencils populated the surface.

The expansive windows, overlooking the locks, allowed plenty of natural light to illuminate the adaptations. Theo grabbed a pencil fragment and sketched in a minor change. "If we don't add that mechanism, there could be problems later – down here." He unrolled the paper further and pointed to the row of valves.

Mr. Sehler scratched his chin. "Right. Get the other engineers in here and let's get this change approved before we send this off to the government."

"Sure thing."

"Say, did you ever find that cup of tea you were looking for?"

Theo groaned. His boss was forever teasing him about his fondness for the English drink. "No. Might find a way to get over to Canada and look."

"My wife recommended a place down near the end of Portage."

"I'll have to take a walk down there after work one day."

Item 1 – Meet with the bank manager and withdraw enough funds to meet your initial week's expenses.

Lilly fulfilled the first part of the item, collecting a sum of money that would have lasted her family two months, not just a week. Then she'd ducked into a restaurant and forced herself to eat slowly. She'd ordered a pasty, which the waitress described as a meat pie. With trembling hands, she'd eaten one bite at a time with her fork instead of lifting it to her lips and devouring the tasty pastry filled with beef and potato chunks, onion bits, sliced carrots, and diced turnips.

The waitress returned with a small bowl of tomato sauce. "Try it with catsup."

"Thank you." After trying the pasty with catsup on it, Lilly knew she'd found a new favorite food.

After paying, and leaving a tip, Lilly headed on to complete the second part of her aunt's request: *Be sure to get enough money to purchase a wardrobe appropriate for the severe weather in the Upper Peninsula. Absolutely no mourning clothing! I am in heaven, dancing with the Lord.*

She'd entered the Northern Railroad Bank expecting to be thrown out, dressed as poorly as she was. But Lilly clutched her carpetbag to her side, strode up to a teller, and soon her bag was filled with enough cash. She could not only to feed herself and purchase clothes but there was enough for all her siblings as well. Her heart seemed about to hammer through the bodice of her thin dress as she stepped out of the building and into the sunlight.

Passersby gawked at Lilly as she held onto the carpetbag for dear life. Yet, what was inside was only a fraction of the money Aunt Lillian had left in her accounts. Forcing herself to slow her pace and her breathing, Lilly finally stopped outside a building. The sign, painted in fancy gold paint on the window announced this establishment as "The Ladies' Apparel Shoppe." She stared in at two actual mannequins outfitted with spring gowns. She'd never seen the like. The pink gauzy gown on the right looked straight from one of a Godey's magazine that Lilly had read on the train. The get up included gloves, a satin purse, matching kid leather boots, a lacy wool shawl, and a broad hat with silk roses affixed to the hat band. The yellow outfit had a lace inset that barely covered the mannequin's bosom. That number was definitely out.

For the first time in the days since she'd begun her railroad trip, her head seemed to have cleared. The thick brew that passed for coffee and the meat pie surely had helped. God had provided. *Thank you Lord.*

The door opened and bells jangled. "May we help you, mademoiselle?" A coiffed dark-haired woman, so petite she stood only as tall as Lilly's shoulder looked up with warm brown eyes.

"I. . ."

"You are looking for something special, *oui*?"

"Uh, yes. . ." No. She wasn't.

The woman took Lilly's free hand. "Come inside out of the chill. The air is cold today, *n'est ce pas*?"

Inside, Lilly found herself surrounded not only by frilly gowns but by all manner of unmentionables, some actually displayed in the back. She felt her eyes widen. What kind of place was this? Behind her the doorbells rang out.

Two women entered, their bustles brushing against one of the mannequins and the saleslady rushed over before it fell.

"Sorry!" The taller of the two women assisted the Frenchwoman in righting the display. "I love this ensemble. That's why I came in."

"And I want the yellow."

Both women had accents that Lilly had heard near the cities in Lower Michigan, when stopping at the railroad stations near the capital.

"Splendid!" The saleswoman clapped her hands together. "And since I have your measurements on file, I should be able to have both garments altered by. . . say, next Friday?"

"In time for the Locks Association dinner?" The titian-haired visitor glanced at her friend in triumph.

"You shall be the belles of the night."

Lilly moved toward the back of the store as the proprietor conducted her transaction with the women. Surely there had to be a place with more normal clothing. As soon as was possible, she slipped out of the store, the women too engaged in conversation to notice her departure.

Exhaling in relief, she moved down the sidewalk. *Knauf's Mercantile* the sign announced, three doors down. Sucking in a breath, she strode to the store but when Lilly went to open the door it wouldn't budge. She tried again. Someone behind her cleared his throat.

"Allow me." The deep voice rumbled like the sound of thunder before a summer's shower that would clear the mountain air.

Lilly turned to face the stranger. Elegantly attired in long black wool topcoat, a matching banded hat, and black boots buffed to a shine, the gentleman could have jumped off the pages of The Detroit Free Press advertisement she'd seen the previous day – *What the smart man wears to the opera*. He even sported thick dark hair, like the dandy pictured in the newspaper.

With a quick shove, the man pushed the door open. "It sticks."

Theo rubbed his head. He'd removed his eyeglasses earlier, when the migraine had begun. But his vision wasn't so blurred that he couldn't see the rail-thin auburn-haired woman before him. She could blow away in a stiff Lake Superior breeze.

Theo held the door open for the young woman and looked downward, squinting. With the worn boots, she was probably someone from the lumber camps in town to fetch something for her family. But why the tattered carpet bag? Maybe she needed much on this trip. But the bag already looked heavy.

"Miss, might I assist you?" Although how he'd do so with his vision already shattering into fragments, from his blasted headache was beyond him. Still, he held out his hand to take her bag.

The woman clutched her possessions to her calico-covered bosom.

With the squiggly white lines interrupting his vision he couldn't make out her features well. Even in this awful state, though, Theo could take in the shopper's thick wavy hair streaming down her back like an unfettered waterfall. What was her situation?

A sales clerk strode toward them, his bald pate marking him as Mr. Wiggins. "I have your powders, Mr. Reynolds."

Theo had experienced several dealings with the imperious man, none pleasant. But thank God he'd acquired the potion for his migraine. "Thank you."

The clerk leaned in. "Are you with this woman?"

His head throbbing, Theo didn't reply.

The clerk wagged a finger at the young woman. "We don't allow any soliciting in this establishment."

"I don't know what that means, mister, but I got a big list of things I need to buy." She reached into the bag and pulled out an envelope stuffed with something green. *Cash?* "My Aunt Lillian instructed me to get warm clothes."

The young woman's soft southern twang surprised Theo.

Mr. Wiggins gaped, fishlike, at the envelope, before he grabbed the carpetbag. "This is going behind the counter for safekeeping, miss. Now follow me."

Before she could protest, the salesman waved his hand overhead at another employee, bent over a table of cloth. As ornery as the clerks could be in this mercantile, they were always fair, never cheated anyone. The young woman would be well looked after by the staff.

Mr. Wiggins returned to him and gently took Theo's elbow and led him to a chair. "Thank you for bringing your friend in, Mr. Reynolds. Let's get your powders."

"Thank you." Theo sat and the clerk departed.

In less than a minute, the man returned with a small box of powders, each in their own packet. Although Theo couldn't make out the writing on the blue inked labels, he knew they must say "Goodhearts Migraineur powders — Highly effective!!!"

Mr. Wiggins pressed a cup of water into his hand. "Take one now before you head home. We'll see to your lady friend and I'll have her escorted back. Don't worry."

Theo started to shake his head, and state that that wasn't his lady friend but the crushing sensation at his temples allowed no such thing.

Item two — check into the Hotel Iroquois for the first night. Pay in advance. Then make sure the stables know you are in town. Establish an account under your own name. Bring paperwork to show that you own Earl and Duke, as well as my carriage.

Lilly reread the list. She had horses? Surely Earl and Duke wouldn't be at the stable with a carriage if they weren't horses. How would she pay for them? Or feed them? Excitement warred with her practical nature. Her hands trembled. She had horses, a carriage, and a way to feed them. God had provided. She wanted to see the animals and the conveyance.

It wouldn't do any harm to stop there first would it? But with the mercantile delivering all her items, she'd best register as a guest first at the inn.

Lilly ducked into the hotel, its dark green awning stamped *Hotel Iroquois* in white glossy letters. After making her reservations, Lilly headed in the direction of the stables, which the clerk indicated were two blocks south.

Horses! Her own. And a carriage! And new clothes. How thrilling! Although bone weary, Lilly beamed as she strode on, giving her old boots their final workout before they'd be headed for the trash bin.

Leon's Livery. This was the place.

A burly dark-haired man, who reminded her of her Christy cousins, leaned against a pine countertop. "Can I help you?"

She pulled her papers from her bag. "I'm here for Earl and Duke and my Aunt Lillian's carriage."

Twin black eyebrows rose over dark eyes. "Sorry for your loss, miss. Lill was a great lady."

She ducked her chin. "Thank you."

When she looked up he was perusing her papers. He tapped his index finger on them. "Put these away and let me bring them out for you."

She opened her mouth to protest, for she didn't wish to drive the animals down unknown streets but the man had departed quicker than a shot.

The flimsy wood door to the livery opened behind her. The handsome man from the mercantile, face pale, took two steps in before sinking into an oak chair. He rested his head in his hands. "I need a taxi."

Lilly exhaled a long puff of air. What should she say? Or do? "Are you ill?" He'd seemed to be, at the store.

"No." He moaned. "Yes. A headache."

The livery owner returned. "Your horse and carriage will be up front in a moment, miss. Jesse is getting them ready for you."

Before she could protest, he'd turned his gaze to the visitor. "Theo, what's wrong? I ain't got a taxi right now, sorry."

Theo struggled to his feet. "I'll walk then."

"No, wait." Lilly touched the livery owner's sleeve. "I don't need the carriage right now. Could Jesse take this man home?"

"You sure?" Leon scratched his chin.

"Yes. I have more errands near here and won't need the carriage until an hour or so from now."

"All right then. That suit you, Theo?"

Theo squinted up at Lilly. "Thank you, miss."

"Drink some chamomile tea when you get home." She resisted the urge to wag a finger at him as she would with her sisters. Even with a headache, this fellow was the best looking example of manhood she'd ever seen.

"I took a double packet of Goodhearts' powders." He pressed his eyes tightly shut.

"The chamomile will relax you and help you rest." She kept her voice firm. "A good cup of tea will go a long way to helping that headache."

This day was getting stranger and stranger. Theo hadn't even gotten the name of the young woman who'd leant him her carriage and horses – a pair who looked familiar to him, even in Theo's altered state. And while she was a little bossy acting, her heart seemed in the right place, unlike many of the young women with whom he'd grown up. What was her situation? Even with his throbbing head, he discerned she wasn't under a man's protection – which she should be.

Jesse pulled up beside the boarding house and set the brake. "We're here. Do you need help in?"

"No, thanks." Theo stepped down from the open buggy. "Jesse, who was that lady?"

"Don't rightly know." Jesse laughed. "She's quite a looker even in those shabby clothes, ain't she?"

"I didn't get a good look at her." With the squiggly white lines interrupting his vision he couldn't make out her features well. Theo lifted his hand to cover his eyes from the sun.

"Trust me, she's a gem." The horses shook their bridles as though disagreeing with Jesse.

"Regardless, I'm concerned."

"She's new in town and no father with her or husband is what Leon told me."

Theo stepped aside as two of his fellow boarders, both burly men, approached on the walkway. He dipped his chin at the brothers who had left the lumber camps to work as carters at the railroad station.

Theo rubbed his head. "Keep watch over her, Jesse. I can't comment as to her looks, not with this infernal headache but even in a town as safe as this one. . ."

"Yes sir, I understand. Leon and me are gonna check on her each time she sends for her horses."

"And how often might that be?" What if she left only once a week? Theo felt in his coat pocket for a dollar coin. He handed it to the driver. "Let me know where she's staying."

"She's at the Iroquois right now. But I think she might be going on to her aunt's place after that. Ya can't miss it if you walk to the end of Portage. It's a three story building made of that old brick from around these parts."

"Thanks."

The carriage departed and Theo strode toward the white clapboard two-story building that was his temporary home. He was halfway up the broad steps to the porch when the front door opened.

"You've a letter from your dear mother." Mrs. Wilburn's too-loud voice rang in his ears.

From the corner of his blurred vision he saw her waving the missive. What would his mother complain about this time? Theo wasn't in the mood for it.

"You're sick, aren't you?"

"Yes. A migraine."

The plump woman joined him on the stairs and took his arm. "Bedtime for you."

He recalled the newcomer's suggestion. Couldn't hurt to try. "Do you have any chamomile tea, Mrs. Wilburn?"

"I do."

"Might I have some?"

"Certainly. Didn't your Goodhearts come?"

"They did, but. . ." Somehow the strange woman's arrival in the Soo reminded him of a top he'd made as a child. His sisters had insisted that on each side he'd write something silly on it having to do with love. Why did he suddenly feel like a top being spun and wondering on which side he'd land?

"Come on." His landlady cocked her head at him. "You definitely seem out of sorts. A cup of chamomile might be just the thing."

Tea and some time with a stranger who possessed a good heart might heal him even quicker. But for now, he'd have to settle.

Chapter 2

Lilly had checked off most of the items on Aunt Lillian's list before she'd returned to the stables and asked Jesse to drive her home. As she approached the carriage, Lilly appraised the matched pair of bays. Both looked healthy, their coats shiny and well kept. How amazing that she now owned not one horse but two. And a beautiful carriage.

After turning onto Portage Street, Lilly watched, waiting to see the beautiful home Aunt Lill had mentioned in her letters. Jesse directed the horses to pull the smart-looking carriage to the curb and then assisted her out. "Good day, miss."

"Thank you." Lilly smoothed out the wrinkles from her dress the best she could.

Jesse pointed to the house, edged by a fence, just beyond where they'd stopped. "That's it."

As he set off, Lilly stepped onto the boardwalk.

A man, whose pudgy features matched those of the dog he walked, drew closer until he stopped beside her. "Sit!"

Was he talking to her or his pet? Lilly's shoulders stiffened.

His pooch sat, and the clean-shaven man looked up at her. Although she wasn't overly tall, with the heeled boots she'd purchased Lilly stood at least several inches above the stranger.

"Are you Lillian's niece?" He sniffed, as though she might have stepped in some of the manure left behind in the streets.

Sure was strange having unknown folks just walking up and yammering at her. "Yes, sir, I am." She drew up straighter.

"I hope you can get rid of some of that clutter she has in there."

If she'd bought one of those doll-sized parasols she'd seen at the mercantile, Lilly would have been tempted to rap this offensive man with it. Still, maybe he knew something she didn't know. At home there had been little to keep clean, with their small house. But this home looked very large.

"How do you know?"

"I live two houses down."

She puffed out a breath of air. It wouldn't do to already get into arguments with the neighbors. She kept her tone light, "That's an awful lot to keep clean for a widow on her own."

"Humph." The man's snort accompanied his frown. "I hope you'll do better."

He seemed quite serious. Lilly cringed as dread prickled her skin. What was she in for? Rats? Worse?

The neighbor whistled to his dog and then strode off, turning at the corner, and telling the dog, "Heel!"

Lilly flinched and then opened the latch on the gate and entered onto a bricked walkway, which someone had swept clean. She turned and shut the gate again. Someone had taken care of the garden with its low clipped hedges and rose bushes in front of the home. No weeds in sight. Did the attorney say Aunt Lill had a gardener? She couldn't remember. Lilly's hands shook as she approached the steps to the porch of the home on Portage Avenue. This stately three-story home, with its wide, covered front porch was hers?

Lilly fumbled through her reticule until she located the key. She took two steps up onto the wide porch that surrounded the first floor. Wicker settees flanked each side of the double mahogany doors. The benches were topped by blue and cream toile cushions. A wicker side table was set beside each settee. On the far end of the wide-planked porch's expanse hung a swing. It looked straight out of a picture book.

Lilly pressed a hand to her chest, feeling her heart beat rapidly against the new lace-trimmed blouse she'd bought. A chill wind stirred her new burgundy wool skirt and she clutched her coat closer and then headed to the door to unlock it.

Home? Would it be a home without her loved ones there to share it with her?

"Theodore, someone is here to see you." Melvin Dickerson, his supervisor at the Locks waggled his eyebrows. "Keep it short, eh? He's waiting in the front reception room."

Frowning, Theo pushed the diagrams aside that he'd been pouring over all morning. The "reception room" was really a place where any visitors, with no scheduled appointments, were detained until the engineers could discern their business.

Carrying his cup of tea, Theo sipped as he trod down the long hallway. He opened the door to the square room. Inside, the lone "guest" was Jesse.

The stableboy shot to his feet and wrung his cap between his hands. "She was stayin' at the Iroquois but now she's all alone at her aunt's house."

Theo fished a coin out of his vest pocket and flipped it to the young man. "Thank you."

"She ain't called for her horses and carriage yet, either." Jesse wagged his cap in his hands.

Sighing, Theo pulled another coin out and strode to the driver. "Listen, I'm simply expressing my Christian concern for an unaccompanied newcomer to our city. I wouldn't want her to think I was having her followed. That would be untoward. But you're in a position to drive by and check on her, aren't you?"

"Yes, sir. Will do." A huge smile split the driver's face before he turned on his heel and strode off, whistling one of those horrid beer hall ditties.

He should go check on her himself. But they were on a big deadline to get the lock ready. He'd soon be working himself out of a job, when the Army Corps of Engineers took over. Maybe he shouldn't be in such a rush.

"Reynolds?" George Rush called out, down the hall. "You coming?"

Hours later, Theo sat at his desk, sipping the tasteless brew that passed for black tea. He pulled out the missive from his mother and re-read it. Not only was the teacup set "too pinkish" but the Dresden teapot was "too German-looking." It was made in Germany, for heaven's sake! There was no pleasing the woman. Theo crumpled the note from his mother and tossed the note into the trash bin.

George tugged at his tie, loosening it. "What's got you worked up?"

"Can't find the right or shall we say *perfect* teacup for my mother."

"Oh, you should try the Tea Shoppe. I think it's on Portage Avenue."

"The Tea Shoppe?" He frowned. "I've bought fudge down there and a pipe for my father but I've never seen a tea shop."

His colleague lifted his chin, staring upwards for a moment. "Might be up a block or two back from there. Let me ask my wife."

"Thanks."

"She has said they have everything in there that you could want, including that black breakfast tea you've been searching out."

"Wonderful." What would be even better would be if he could find the young woman from the mercantile. She was purported to live on Portage.

"I'm heading for home." George winked at him. "And to my lovely wife."

Fifteen years married, George's enthusiasm for his wife's company never ceased to surprise Theo. Maybe that was because so many of his peers, and his sisters, had married solely for position and money. Thank God he'd fought his mother's insistence that he join his father's business. Where would he be now? He shivered. But he was a self-supporting engineer, praise the Lord.

With his diagrams completed, Theo rolled the plans up and inserted them into their tube, then covered it shut with its metal disk. He departed the stuffy building out into the glorious green grounds that surrounded the Locks. He strode up the street to Portage and then went in look of The Tea Shoppe. This was absolutely the last time he was going to try to find his mother's perfect teacup.

Theo strode past the Fudge Shop, resisting the lure of its tempting scents. Then he passed the tobacconist before the businesses seemed to trickle off and residences dominate, their lawns immaculately mowed, flowers trimmed. Near the end of the block however, a young lad slapped white paint onto the picket fence that surrounded a large three-story establishment – one with several tables on its wide front porch overflowing with teacups and teapots. Jackpot!

He couldn't help grinning. Theo opened the gate and strode up the bricked walkway to the porch. The front door opened and a young woman, attired in a lace and muslin pleated frock stepped out, her ginger upswept hair catching the sunlight. Creamy kidskin boots peeked out beneath the eyelet hem of the flounced skirt. White cotton gloves protected her hands.

"Oh, hello." The woman's breathy voice made it sound as though she knew him.

Was this the same young woman? Theo didn't want to embarrass himself if it wasn't. Regardless, he'd focus on the goal of finding another teacup for his mother – then he'd inquire about Lilly. "I'm so glad to find you here."

The beautiful young woman beamed, her brown eyes widening. "I'm glad to be found."

Was this the bedraggled woman from the mercantile and livery? He'd been so ill when they'd met, and his vision so fragmented, that he'd not gotten a look at anything but her giving spirit and kind soul. Maybe that was what God needed him to see.

Lilly waited expectantly. The man had obviously recovered from his headache. Jesse, at the livery, had told her that Theo had asked about her. She'd assured Jesse she was fine. After all, even though she didn't keep a shotgun, like Mama did at home, her cousins would come check on her soon. And her sisters, Lord willing, would soon be joining her. First she needed to clear the large house of its overflowing collection of teacups, saucers, teapots, and all manner of tea paraphernalia.

Theo tugged at the lapel of his gray suit coat. "I'm looking for the perfect teacup for my mother."

No mention of a *thank you* for the use of the carriage? No, *I'm glad to see you*? "Well, I've got an overabundance for you to look at if you'd like to pick one out." Maybe Mama was wrong about city folk having more manners.

"Thank you." A blush touched the man's high cheekbones. "My supervisor directed me here."

Why would his boss man send Theo here? Was he a salesman? Was this a ploy to get her to buy something? The attorney said to watch out for those types of men. "Oh?"

"Yes, I work at the Locks. I'm an engineer there."

She exhaled in relief, surprised how glad she was that he didn't plan on selling her anything. "How exciting."

"Not nearly as interesting as running a tea shop, I'm sure." He moved further out onto the porch, where she'd been organizing her aunt's collections.

What could she say to that? "I have no idea."

He swiveled toward her, sun illuminating his handsome features and the cleft in his chin. "I can assure you that hours spent pouring over drawings and reading and rereading paperwork can become quite tedious."

"Still, what an accomplishment." She tried to keep the southern twang from her voice, having heard from Leon at the Livery that most northerners didn't cotton to southerners. "Your mother must be…" she caught herself before saying "right proud" and corrected herself, "proud of you."

The good humor on his face fled and he turned to examine another set of porcelain teacups. How could a body use so many teacups in one lifetime? And her aunt a widow woman.

"My mother has yet to find anything to be proud of in anyone besides herself." Although he laughed, Theo's voice held restrained bitterness.

"Oh my. I hope you're not funning me." She covered her mouth. She should have said another word. "Joking?"

He pressed a hand to his vest-covered chest. "I wish I were."

"Hmmm, I'm not sure any of these teacups will please her, then." Lilly picked up a pretty pale green and gold cup with tiny doves painted around the rim. "They're old."

"Old?" He laughed. "You mean antique."

His back was to her, so she wasn't sure if he was mocking her. Yes, the teacups were all old but she'd washed each and every one and dried them. Antique meant really old. Was he insulting her aunt's collection as too old to be worthwhile? Mama nearly wept any time Pa had brought her something new. Would Theo's mother want her son to buy an untouched teacup and saucer from the mercantile? Had he been sending the poor woman things that were secondhand?

He held a blue and white cup aloft and looked at the bottom. "Limoges," he gasped. "And if I'm correct this is from the beginning of the 1800's. My mother would be ecstatic over this."

"You sure your Ma would want that, Theo—it's nearly a hundred years old." Her Kentucky twang could not be stifled.

He faced her, eyebrow raised. "Lilly?"

"You're the fella from the mercantile. You rode home, sick, in my carriage."

"Yes, I'm Theodore Reynolds, but everyone calls me Theo." He set the teacup down. "And your name?"

"Lilly Smith."

"Lilly of the chamomile tea." The silky way he said it, was like the way a poet read verses. A thrill shot through Lilly.

"Did it help?" Her own voice sounded husky.

"Yes." He met and held her gaze. A question seemed to linger there.

"I'm glad." She averted her gaze. She shouldn't be staring at the handsome man like that. She didn't even know him.

"Do you serve it here?"

Serve it? What a way to put it. Serve tea? "I make it up now and again."

He slowly shook his head and then scanned her briefly from head to toe. "All I could see of you the other day were your old boots—which I see you're not wearing today—and your beautiful hair."

He'd called her unruly mop of curls beautiful. Lilly beamed.

His face turned crimson. "I mean, that is, my vision was so obscured from my migraine that was all I could see." If anything, Theo's face reddened further.

Lilly frowned and patted her chignon. "It's easier to work with my hair secured up."

"Yes, well, I can imagine so." He picked the teacup up again. "How much is it for this one?"

"How much?" Lilly blinked.

He reached into his pocket and pulled out some cash.

How embarrassing. Yes, she'd wondered what to do with her aunt's goods but she'd not yet considered selling things off. She'd have to pray about that. Still, with Aunt Lillian's stipulation that none of the bank money's initial withdrawal could be used for anyone but herself, Lilly had wondered how she'd get her sisters up north. Church ladies had stopped the previous night and asked for donations and all Lilly had been able to give them was a dime, not sure if donations would go against her aunt's wishes.

Theo cocked his head at her.

She swallowed. She wasn't used to taking money from anyone. But it wouldn't be for her. Rubbing her arms, she nodded toward a crystal bowl on the center table. "You can put it in there. Take the saucer, too."

"Do you have any bags?"

"Bags?" Why would she? She'd brought only the one carpetbag on her trip.

He waited. "To put them in?"

"Oh! Let me get a little box." She went inside and grabbed one of the many boxes she'd found stacked in a corner. With her handkerchief, she wiped dust from one, on all sides before returning outside.

When she handed him the fancy peach and yellow swirled box, a smile tugged at his lips. "How clever, using a box just like those used at Roquefort's in Detroit."

While traveling on the train, Lilly had heard a matron mention Roquefort's to her daughter as "the place" to register for wedding china. She didn't know how to reply to Theo's comment, as she'd never seen a box from the place. She certainly didn't feel clever, as the handsome man suggested. "I just hope your Mama likes it."

The lilac bushes, along Theo's walk home, leant their heady fragrance as though congratulating him on his good luck. He clutched the fancy box to his chest, tempted to throw his straw boater overhead in celebration. Lilly hadn't departed town. And she ran a tea shop. Which gave him every excuse to return to her establishment frequently. Would tomorrow be too soon?

Soon he neared the rooming house. Mrs. Elsner sat in a chair on the front lawn, watching the street. She gestured for him to sit beside him. "What's got you looking like the Cheshire cat?"

He thrust out the pastel box.

"What's this?"

"An antique teacup and saucer that even my mother can't deny are beautiful." Almost as lovely as the teashop owner.

Mrs. Elsner gingerly opened the box and held up the cup. She drew in a sharp breath. "It's fantastic."

"Nearly a hundred years old, too."

Her eyes grew wide. "Ya don't say."

"Yes, ma'am, if I remember correctly. My grandmother had some like this at her home."

"Doesn't your mother have them now?"

He stifled a snort of derision. His mother's obsession with tea sets had begun when her mother had stipulated in her will that all of her collection of teacups and teapots and the like were to be donated to the local Daughters of the American Revolution chapter to which she belonged. Mother had been furious for weeks. That anger transformed into a cold chill. Then began the demands that her son and daughters find her the most beautiful teacups they could, for any special holiday.

"Where did you buy this?"

"The Tea Shoppe on Portage."

"Nice place but I didn't know they carried anything of this quality." Mrs. Elsner frowned. "And I didn't think they were exactly on Portage. . ."

"Almost at the end of the street." Theo rubbed his chin. There had been no sign, but perhaps Lilly had removed it while cleaning. "I think she was clearing out stock that had been in the attic or some such thing."

"Maybe she'd been holding back some of the better stuff for summer. Vacationers should arrive soon and they'll pay better than locals will."

"I'm going back tomorrow."

"Why?"

To see a brown-eyed beauty. "I want to make sure I look through all of their items, in case Mother doesn't care for this one."

She sighed. "Good idea."

"I'll never tell that Canadian proprietor what she said, either." Theo and Mrs. Elsner had gone to the twin city of Sault Sainte Marie, Ontario to an expensive shop she'd heard about.

His landlady laughed. "I should have sent you to the Tea Shoppe first."

The faint scent of roast beef carried on the breeze. "Dinner smells good."

"Oh my." The sweet-faced lady rose. "I best get that out of the oven.

Theo went inside, allowing himself a moment for his eyes to adjust to the dark interior. He grabbed an oil lamp from a stand and went up the dim stairwell and to his room. This place was so unlike his home outside of Detroit. The descendant of wealthy French merchants, who'd left France after Napoleon's downfall, Theo had been taught to work hard. And from his father's side, American investors with a penchant for gambling on high risk investments and winning, until recently, he'd learned that everything came at a cost. Wouldn't Father be shocked to see Theo brushing off his own suitcoat?

He poured water from the chipped enamel pitcher into the shallow basin. Then he grabbed a cloth, dipped it in the water and then ran it over a bar of the English Lifebuoy soap that Mother claimed had health benefits. After washing up with the carbolic soap, which smelled of coal tar, he patted on some cologne. Then Theo headed down to join the other boarders for dinner. Afterwards, one of the brothers suggested a game of cards while Mrs. Elsner played the piano in the parlor. And for the first time, in all the time he'd been living there, inexplicable loneliness washed over him. And a longing to be spending his evening with Lilly.

Chapter 3

"Theodore? Did you hear the numbers I quoted?" Mr. Dickerson drew in a deep inhalation on his pipe—a sign he was annoyed. Then the supervisor puffed smoke rings up to the paneled ceiling. The golden oak finish appeared grayish above the man's usual seat, stained by his habit.

"I was thinking about. . ." While Theo's mind was normally occupied by numbers and charts, the image of Lilly's sweet face was the only thing he'd contemplated all morning.

The youngest engineer, Franz Klassen, steepled his fingers together. "He's distracted by something."

"Or someone." George Rush winked. "Someone from the Tea Shoppe?"

Their superior waggled his eyebrows. "Enough of that, let's pay attention to why or why not this system will work with these changes."

The four men bent over the diagram that stretched out on the rectangular work table. After much debate, and Theo rubbing his stiff neck, they'd reached a consensus. It wouldn't work.

"Back to rework the calculations." Klassen sighed. Being the latest hire, he usually was tasked to redo the numbers.

Theo drew in a deep breath and inhaled. As he returned to his desk, he withdrew his pocket watch from his vest. The deer's head, engraved into the gold piece, reminded him of the trips he and Father had made together. They'd hunt not far from where Theo now worked. Those trips had given him a love of the north woods.

"Coffee?" The coffee girl walked by with a tray loaded with German pastries, from her nearby shop.

"Wish you'd bring us tea." As soon as the words left his lips, Theo regretted his grumbling. "Sorry, it doesn't make sense to do that."

The tiny blonde flicked her long braid over her shoulder. "Did you ever find that strong English brew you wanted?"

"No." Did Lilly carry it?

"I'll get my mother to order some through the store." Married, with three children, the woman wasn't much older than Theo.

"Thank you."

"Try the strudel. I made it this morning." Her blue eyes widened. "My *kinder* love it."

"I'm sure I will, too. Thank you."

He followed her to the staff room. A small bouquet of garden roses sat surrounded by all manner of pastries. "Those flowers are pretty."

"Thank you. I picked them from our garden. Our early roses."

Mother would have turned up her nose at the casual arrangement of the lilacs and roses. Only hothouse flowers, professionally arranged would do for her.

George joined him and grabbed up a Danish dotted with cream cheese. "I say we test the system soon before we go any further with those calculations."

A test? They performed them often enough.

"Good thing my wife didn't perform any system stress tests on me before we married." George tugged on his lapel, plucked a single rose blossom from the arrangement and pushed it through, patting it. "I'd not have passed the test, yet here we are fifteen years later."

Franz guffawed. "If you can manage two sets of twins and three more children during that time, I'd say you've passed the fatherhood stress test!"

Lilly wasn't a hothouse flower type. Was she? Maybe his landlady would help him put his question to the test. He grinned, imaging his hoped-for reaction.

After work, and fetching a bouquet from the rooming house's backyard garden, with Mrs. Elsner's permission, Theo strode off to the tea shop. What would her reaction be?

As he approached, he spied her sweeping the front porch, curls drooping around her pretty face, the rest of her hair wrapped in some kind of scarf. She'd scare off customers if she waited on them attired in the tattered dress she wore and appearing so disheveled. Despite her attire, though, her loveliness shone through.

"Lilly?" He held out the bouquet as he approached.

Lilly pressed a hand to her cheek. Perspiration glinted on her forehead as she set the broom aside. A minute passed before she took the flowers. She stared at them, a perplexed expression on her face.

He'd failed. She didn't like them and didn't know what to say. "They're from my landlady's garden."

Puffing out a breath, Lilly sank into a nearby chair. A different array of teacups and saucers were neatly arranged on the table beside her. "Well, I never. . ."

Lilly pressed a hand to her chest. Was a man—this man—actually bringing her flowers? She gestured to the chair on the other side of the small table, covered by that day's assortment of teacups.

Theo's grin faltered. "I thought these would look nice on one of your tables."

"Thank you." She inhaled the flower's fragrance and smiled. What was one supposed to say when receiving flowers? Thank you didn't seem enough.

"Do you have a vase?" He remained standing, looking down at her.

Should she stand back up? No, if she did, she might collapse. She was too exhausted to look through any more of Aunt Lillian's overstuffed closets to find a vase, although it seemed she'd seen one somewhere.

He glanced around. "Maybe putting some flowers in vases out here would draw more customers."

"Customers?"

"For your wares." He cocked his head to the side in such an adorable manner that she couldn't correct him.

"Ah, well, you're my only so-called customer." She chuckled. What a strange sense of humor this man had.

His forehead crinkled. "Busy earlier?"

"I'm slap wore out, if you want the truth." She blew out a puff of air, causing a stray curl on her forehead to bob.

"Why not let me help?"

Lilly pulled a rose from the bouquet. "Why don't we cut these and fill the cups with water?"

"That's an idea. Where is your aunt's shed? I'll go get some snips."

"It's in the back." Lilly lifted a lilac to her nose and inhaled. "They smell so lovely."

Theo grinned down at her before he scrambled down the steps, and around the side of the house like one of her young cousins might, back home.

Lilly felt in her apron for the letter from home. Even though Mama was feeling better, she wanted Lilly's oldest sisters to come up North with her. Would Daisy and Delphinium mind her? Was Mama truly well now that the specialist had seen her?

Her cousin Garrett and his wife and children would be coming to visit soon. They would take many of Aunt Lillian's collection over to Mackinac Island for their tea shop. How funny that Theo seemed to think this house was a shop. No sense disappointing the handsome young man. She rose and went inside to start the tea kettle.

She entered the house, cool and dim. She got the stove going and pumped water into the kettle before setting it back on the fancy new stove from Detroit. Aunt Lillian had written of it in her letters to Mama, but Lilly had never seen anything like it in her life and it had taken a bit of time to get accustomed to it.

"Lilly?" Theo rapped on the screen door frame. "I couldn't find the cutters."

She went back to the front and opened the door. "Come on back. I have kitchen scissors that should do and I know I saw a vase somewhere."

Sunlight streamed through the large side windows in the foyer as she led him through, to the kitchen. She dare not open the cabinets on the right, which were crammed with teapots and teacups. Instead she went to the left side, which she'd already organized. "Hand me the stepladder, please."

Theo opened it and set the stepladder beneath the tall cabinets. "I see it up there. Let me get it."

Soon he'd retrieved a creamy milkware vase painted with roses and camellias. He glanced around the large room. "Did she serve in her parlor, in the winter?"

Was he hinting at wanting dinner? "I'm not sure, but probably so."

He returned the stepstool to its place. His stomach growled.

Lilly couldn't repress her laugh. "Would you like to stay for supper? It's almost time."

In the parlor, the grandfather clock chimed, as if in agreement.

"How about some fried chicken?"

"Fried chicken?" His face screwed up, as if in confusion.

"Well, I'd have greens, taters and gravy, and I've already got biscuits made—so you won't go hungry."

His Adam's apple bobbed. "Sounds lovely."

"It'll take a while." She was so excited about what awaited in her icebox. "But I have to tell you something I am so thrilled about."

"What's that?"

"I didn't have to pluck the chicken nor did I have to cut off the darned thing's head!"

Theo felt his eyebrows must have launched clear up to his hairline. Having grown up in a household where the closest he'd gotten to a chicken was at dinner, dressed for the occasion, and cook and the servants having prepared it. "I'm so happy for you." What else could he say?

Lilly beamed at him. "I thought you might be. You seem to be such a nice down-to-earth fellow."

Was he? Mother would have been appalled to know he'd be eating what she considered Southern fare, never served at her table, ever.

"How can I help?"

"Do you know how to cook?"

"No."

She grinned again, sending warmth through him. "Then you best stay out of the way. That's how you could help."

"All right." He sat at a high backed rush-seated chair. "Say, have you thought about doing something about that back garden area? Maybe serving tea out there?"

He'd spied a beautiful old structure at the far reach of the garden. It had fallen into disrepair, a though neglected for years, despite the care the garden, itself, appeared to have had. His great-grandparents had a large similar-looking garden feature which they called a folly, but it was built from marble or stone. Theo had spent many an afternoon in that pretty outdoor shelter, imagining the day when he'd be an engineer, building great ships — never imagining he'd help with the mechanisms that moved those vessels from one body of water to another.

Lilly set a large iron skillet on the stove top. "It is right pretty out there, isn't it?"

"That's what I thought when I went to the shed. If you had a screen put up between that and the garden, and added some gravel around the side of the house, I think you could attract folks to the back garden." And if someone would either repair or replace the folly.

"It would take an awful lot of work." She removed the chicken from the icebox and brought it to the counter.

"But it would be so lovely." But Theo's talents weren't well-developed in constructing things. Rather, he told others how to build things, such as changes in the Locks.

"Truth be told, I haven't spent much time out there. I've been too busy with the. . .inventory." Her pretty lips drew into a purse expression, as though she wanted to say something more.

"Yes, I suppose that has to be done." Every business owner certainly must keep up with their paperwork.

She made no reply, turning her back to him momentarily.

He might not be able to make large repairs, but certainly he could do something. "I could help you with it."

"With what?" She rolled the chicken pieces in flour and then sprinkled pepper and salt on them.

"The garden."

"Oh."

Not that he knew much about gardening, other than tagging along after their gardener. "If I'm not imposing, that is."

She laughed. "You're my first friend here, Theo. You can impose all you'd like."

Her friend? He longed to be more.

Soon the scent of fried chicken filled the room. She boiled the already-peeled potatoes and chopped some dark green leaves before dousing them with vinegar and cooking them in another pot.

Later, after consuming far more delicious chicken than he should have, Theo patted his stomach. Lilly had far surpassed any test he could have given. Could he pass any she gave him? He wasn't so sure.

A trio of well-dressed women stopped at Lilly's gate. She continued checking the bottoms of the cups and recording their descriptions and the imprint on her notepad. She was now up to over two hundres sets. How could one woman have so many? Perhaps Aunt Lillian had intended to set up shop. But how could Lilly find out? The neighbors hadn't exactly been swarming the place with condolences or welcomes.

The three trod up the walkway. The two younger women twirled small pastel parasols over their heads. All wore white gloves, despite the warm day. Lilly glanced down at her own chafed hands and clasped them together. "Hello."

All glanced between one another and then they each scanned the beautiful house, the lawn, and the tables on the porch covered with tea sets. "We don't see your sign."

Sign? Several of the cottages further along had sweet names like "Nonni's Treasures" which she assumed meant the white-haired woman's grandchildren, as she had many at her home every day. How had Aunt Lillian referred to her home? Was it some Northern eccentricity?

Lilly blinked at them. "I don't have one, but I'm fixin' to." Just as soon as she asked Theo where she could get one made.

"Oh!" The woman with salt-and-pepper hair, upswept under a fashionable little befeathered cap, seemed relieved.

The two other ladies smiled.

"Might we look?"

When they pointed to the porch and the teacups, Lilly nodded. "Sure thing. I'm trying to get these out of here to make room." For her sisters. But these strangers didn't need to know that.

"We're Mrs. Rush, Mrs. Klassen, and Mrs. Dickerson. Theo sent us."

"Oh." She smiled. "Any friend of Theo is a friend of mine. Welcome."

"Thank you."

"He said you had an amazing assortment and he was right."

"He's such a dear." The youngest one, her hair swept up in a fashionable style, barely looked out of her teen years.

"So hard working." The woman, about thirty or so judging from her appearance, while pretty also had dark rings under her eyes.

"And thoughtful of his mother." The dark-haired matron adjusted the waistband of her skirt, beneath her too tightly fitted navy jacket. "In fact that's why he's been coming over here."

"Oh?" A rock seemed to have plummeted into her gut. "Is that so?"

"Yes. He's been trying to find just the right teacup and saucer that will please her." She arched an eyebrow.

So that was what he was up to. And now three strange women were marching up to her new home, just as pretty as you please, acting like they owned the place. Lilly's ire rose. "She sounds like such a bitty, if you ask me."

The older woman raised an eyebrow. "Mrs. Archibald Reynolds may be a bitty, but with her fortune, that might account for her demeanor."

Lilly ran her tongue over her upper lip. "Theo's family is wealthy?"

Mrs. Rush clasped her hands at her waist. "We've wondered what he is doing working as an engineer, since we found out."

The older woman made a buttoning motion over her mouth. "Melvin told me that, I probably shouldn't have repeated it."

"But it is so delicious to think of one of the Locks' engineers hailing from such a prominent family." Mrs. Klassen's girlish giggle seemed out of place. "He puts on no airs."

"He certainly doesn't." Mrs. Dickerson lifted her chin. "And lives so frugally."

Lilly's head began to ache. No rich educated man was going to have any genuine interest in her. She drew in a long slow breath and exhaled.

"I'd like these." The matron lifted two pretty yellow tea cups and saucers from where they sat on a table. "Could you box them up?" The woman turned to Lilly, as though she was a servant. Was that how Theo saw her?

She crossed her arms. "They aren't for sale."

The three exchanged incredulous looks with one another. "I'm real particular who gets Aunt Lillian's stuff." And these three gossipy women weren't.

"What?" Mrs. Klassen squeaked.

She didn't even know these women, who'd waltzed right up and started grabbing at things. "I apologize. I'm afraid I was wrong."

"About?" Mrs. Rush's perplexed face held sympathy.

"Either you're not friends of Theo's or maybe any friend of his ain't my friend. Now scat." She motioned for the women to move on.

"Scat?" Mrs. Klassen's youthful voice rose.

"You've done wore out your welcome here." Lilly repeated Pa's phrase. In the mountains, that intonement was often accompanied by hoisting the shotgun from the wall.

"Well, I never!" Mrs. Reynolds grabbed a fold of her dark bombazine skirt, and swiveled away from Lilly.

As the three women stalked off, Lillian decided on her first purchase. A rocking chair. She'd not rock in it with a shotgun across her lap, like Pa had done, but she sure as shootin' wasn't gonna keep having strangers moseying up to her house thinking they could walk off with Aunt Lillian's goods.

Chapter 4

Theo whistled *Beautiful Dreamer* as he walked home along Bingham. The parlor song, published after Stephen Foster's death, had been one of Father's favorites and one Theo's landlady played often. Soon, he turned down the boarding house street and arrived home. Mrs. Elsner sat out front, shucking peas into a bowl. She wiped her hands off and pulled a yellow envelope from her apron pocket.

"Here you go, Theodore. A letter from your sister, I believe."

He stopped whistling. "I hope you're wrong."

Edwina didn't write unless she wanted something or had unpleasant news. He accepted the missive, sank down on the steps beside the boarding house owner, and opened the letter.

Dearest Teds,

I wanted to write to warn you that Mother plans to stop at your place next. Never mind that I told her you still write from a boarding house address, she INSISTS that since she TOLD you to obtain a rental house for her for the summer that you'll have done so.

Theo dropped the letter into his lap as a fly buzzed past them. He shooed it away.

"What is it?" Mrs. Elsner stopped shelling the peas again.

"My mother." He owed his mother honor, but did God really believe Theo owed her a house rented for the summer?

"She isn't. . ." His landlady's pale eyes widened. She knew about Mother's demand.

"She is."

"Oh no." One pudgy hand flew to her flushed face. "You know I have no room for her here. And. . ."

Theo cleared his throat and interrupted. He knew what she was thinking. That it would be far too humble for his mother's tastes, despite her current circumstances, which Mother apparently failed to accept. "I know. I understand."

"What will you do?" Her blond eyebrows knit together.

"I don't know." He was only an engineer, not a supervisor or manager. "My income only stretches so far and I've needed to put aside for my own future."

He'd dreamed of one day providing a home for a wife and children. That day, which had seemed far off, now loomed closer since he'd met Lilly. But now he'd have to dip into his savings. He'd be the first Reynolds in four generations forced to purchase his own home instead of inheriting or being gifted with a country estate. He picked up the letter and read on.

Teds, Mother also said something I want to share with you. She said you were RIGHT to disobey her all those years ago. She said "Thank God, your brother had the good sense to ignore my instruction." Can you believe that? In any event, I cannot convince her to stay with us in Syracuse. The summer season is upon us and she frets that someone will discover her true state of affairs, which dear brother, are yours as well. Do not fear, though, she intends to rotate between Nanette and myself and our husbands are quite content to have Grandmother come visit with the children.

Love and prayers (you will NEED them!), Your loving sister, Edwina

A young boy, perhaps no more than ten or eleven, rode his bicycle up the road and then veered toward their yard. "Telegram!"

Theo and Mrs. Elsner exchanged a knowing glance. Only one person ever sent a telegram – his mother. He rubbed a spot on his scalp that had begun to throb.

After tipping the boy, Theo read the telegram aloud. "Arriving on train by Saturday. Mother."

"That's it?"

"Yes." How much had that cost her? Father's fiscal irresponsibility had cost Mother most of all. But now Theo would be paying for it. What could he do?

"Do you know anyone who might be letting out rooms, since the cost of a rental house is so dear?"

"No, but. . ." Dare he? How could he ask Lilly this favor when she'd only met him a week earlier?

Lilly had worked herself up into quite a dither after the women left. Not only was her sisters' room clean as a whistle but the other two on that hall were also freshened and neat. Thankfully, she'd already boxed and packed up a hundred teacups and saucers for her cousin, Garrett, to take back to Mackinac Island for his wife's tea shop. He should be there any time. She had to take a quick bath before the late train arrived. What an unbelievable pleasure it had been to enjoy her first bath in the huge porcelain tub. Indoor plumbing! What a luxury. She started the water, pouring in some of her aunt's rose perfumed oil. She needed to still get rid of that last bit of steam she'd worked up over those ladies.

"Hello the house. It's Garrett Christy!" Her cousin's deep voice boomed from the front door.

"Garrett! I'll be right down." She turned off the faucets.

Lilly scurried down the steps. It had been years since she'd seen him, although Mama had received a photograph of Garrett and his wife, Rebecca Jane. She stopped descending the stairs when she caught sight of him. This was no boy. He was a full-grown and very handsome man. Nearly-black hair curled around his forehead, matched by his dark eyes. Even standing a tread up, he was taller than her.

He stepped forward and pulled her into a quick embrace. "Little Lilly--look at you!"

She stepped down and looked up at him. "Maybe I should have stayed on the stairs. And you're a grown up man now. I'm so glad to see you."

He ducked his chin. "Sorry my sweetheart ain't here, but she's feelin' a might poorly."

"Oh?"

His cheeks reddened. "We're hopin' for a Christmas gift."

"A baby?" A thrill shot through her. What would it be like to know you were going to be adding to a family you loved? "Congratulations."

"Thanks." He set his carpetbag down on the floor. "Do I hear water runnin'?"

Lilly's hands flew to her mouth. "Yes, I was just about to take a bath."

"Don't let me keep you. You go on up and take care of all that. I'm early. I reckon if you point me to the water, I can drink me a glass and rock on your porch."

"Rock?"

"Yes, ma'am. Ya don't think I came empty-handed now did ya?" Garrett gave her a half-smile, like he had a secret.

Lilly peeked outside at the gorgeous oak rocker. She gasped. "I heard from Mama that you were quite the craftsman now, but I had no idea."

His high cheekbones turned a rosy shade. "The folks at the Grand Hotel like my work. As does Rebecca Jane. So maybe I'm a fair woodworker."

"Fair? I'd say extremely talented. I've never seen one so pretty." She touched the satin-smooth back. "I love it."

He beamed and Lilly gave him another quick hug.

"You go on now, Little Lil, and get your bath and I'll break it in for ya."

"Are you sure?" She hated leaving him downstairs by himself when he'd just arrived.

"Sure as shootin'."

"Thank you, Garrett." She pointed to the kitchen. "Glasses are on the left and the pump works fine, no trouble."

"Good, thanks."

"If a dark-haired young man comes by, please tell him to wait." She had something to say to him.

"Sure thing." Garrett's dark brows drew together. "This fella got a name?"

"Theo."

"Ah." A gleam lit his dark eyes. "Now you go scoot."

She giggled and headed up the stairs. After grabbing her robe and an extra towel for her hair, which sorely needed a washing, Lilly entered the bathroom and climbed into the tub.

Although she'd love to relax, she tried to accomplish her ablutions as quickly as she could. Two men's voices collided downstairs. Who was Garrett speaking with? Or was it her imagination?

Theo hurried to Lilly's tea shop. A good cup of strong tea, or even the sassafras she brewed, might help him think more clearly. Somehow, talking with her made things seem to work out better. As he neared the three story establishment, he spied a dark-haired man rocking on the porch. Theo stopped cold in his tracks. Two women approached on the walkway, both with skirts wide enough to sweep one another from the walkway, yet they managed to stride side-by-side. He stepped off the sidewalk, onto the grass and turned sideways to allow the women by. Both cast their eyes downward as he were beneath their attention. He'd noticed that most married women in the town had this manner of interaction with men outside of church, their homes, or social situations. A married woman gave no other man except her husband any attention whatsoever. How very different from his parents' social circle in New York, where scandals continued to crop up over marital infidelities. At least his father hadn't done that, as far as Theo knew.

When they passed, Theo continued on, but more slowly. Although the man in the chair didn't wear the clothing of a lumberjack, he looked like one, with a brawny build. The stranger wore the plain clothing of a working man, including suspenders that only emphasized the breadth of his shoulders. He required no arm garters for his sleeves as his bulky muscles and long arms filled out the extra-long sleeves of a store-purchased, rather than tailored, shirt.

Even a workingman might wish to buy teacups for his lady, mightn't he? Theo hesitated before pushing through the gate.

As he approached the porch, the man rose, his height well over six feet tall. "Howdy. You lookin' for Lilly?"

Dust seemed to clog Theo's throat. "Yes."

"She's takin' a bath. Reckon she's tryin' to look pretty for someone." The man winked.

Was this rough character, who Theo had to admit was a striking-looking man, Lilly's sweetheart? "Oh, well, I'll leave you two to. . ."

To what? She was upstairs in the bath while this man was downstairs. Only someone who was very close, or even intimate with someone did that. His face heated.

"You Theo?" The big man cracked his knuckles.

"Uh, yes." Good heavens, did the man intend to hit him?

Stretching his arms out one way and then another, the man's dark eyes appraised him. "You sweet on her?"

"Uh. . ."

The door flew open. With a towel wrapped around her head and covered in a too-large winter robe, Lilly peered out through a crack in the door. Beside her, on the floor, was the telling bulge of a suitcase. This man was staying here.

"I'll be on my way." Theo turned away.

"Theo!" Lilly's voice pinned him there but he didn't turn. "I need to talk with you."

"Come on back here and sit a spell and tell me all about yourself." The man laughed. He had the audacity to laugh at Theo.

"Garrett Christy!" Lilly's aggrieved tone sounded much like his sisters' did when Theo had offended.

"Ya ain't got any brothers here to protect ya so I guess a cousin will have to do."

Her cousin? Theo inhaled the sweet fragrance of a nearby rose bush as he slowly swiveled around.

"If ya sit down by me I'll show ya some pictures of my sweetheart, too." Garrett reached into his lightweight poplin coat and drew out a small leather encased photograph. "And my children."

"I want to see that, Garrett." Lilly stepped onto the porch in her bare feet.

Garrett waved a beefy hand. "Get on back upstairs and get dressed before I force this fella to marry you after seein' ya like that. Don't forget about Jo and Tom and all the trouble Moose and I gave those two."

"I heard about your antics from Mama," Lilly grumbled, before she slammed the door shut.

Theo approached the porch and heard the patter of her feet up the steps. Another door slammed

"She's got a bit of a temper," Garrett drawled.

Theo laughed. "Does she now?"

By the time Lilly came down, about a half hour later, Theo had learned about Lilly's family including cousins, aunts, uncles, grandparents, and all about their life in Kentucky and the cousins' upbringing in lumber camps.

"I don't usually talk this much." Garrett rubbed his chin. "It's just. . . I got a feelin' about you and Lilly."

"A feeling?"

"Can't explain it, but. . ."

The door swung open again. This time Lilly's damp hair was secured up, looped loosely, with pins. She wore a muslin dress that emphasized her form and pretty coloring. "I'm taking you two fellas out tonight."

"To a restaurant?" Garrett's skeptical tone was accompanied by a faint scowl. "This here is a single fella. Dontcha know he probably eats out a lot. Plus a lady doesn't take a fella out. It's the other way around."

Lilly scowled at her cousin. "Same old bossy Garrett."

"Same old silly Lilly."

They each threw playful fake swats at one another and laughed.

"I do have another idea." Mrs. Elsner had encouraged him to invite Lilly for dinner sometime. Since three of the boarders had gone home for the weekend she'd likely not mind these two at the table. And he'd compensate his landlady for the cost.

"As long as we have a little time to speak tonight." Her voice held an edge he'd not heard before.

"I apologize for making a nuisance of myself."

Garrett laughed. "The only way you'll make headway with a Christy or a Christy cousin is to make a nuisance of yourself."

Exhaling a puff of air, Lilly glared at her cousin. "Are you tryin' to wear out your welcome right quick?"

The thickness of her accent recollected the day of her arrival. "As long as I get to speak with you, too, Miss Smith."

Lilly picked at her food. The other boarders had left the table, giving the four of them some privacy in the gas-lit room, with a fancy chandelier hanging over the table. The landlady knew Theo well. He'd boarded there several years. She tried to be quiet lest she say something wrong. And she wanted to hear more of Mrs. Elsner's comments. She especially wanted to know why the woman implied that Theo's mother rotated between her daughter's homes. But if she was wealthy, or at least prominent, why didn't she have her own home?

"These victuals are right good." Garrett grinned at Theo's landlady, who continued to wear the bemused expression she'd had when he'd brought them there.

"Thank you, Mr. Christy. I imagine it is nothing compared to eating at the Grand Hotel."

"The Grand Hotel does have some mighty fine fixin's." Garrett nodded and bent over his plate. He still consumed as much as a lumberjack. How did he stay so trim?

"Theo is my most thoughtful boarder." Mrs. Elsner dabbed at her mouth with her napkin. "And he's the only one I've had who worked on the locks."

On locks? Lilly glanced across the table at Theo, who was serving himself another slice of chocolate cake. "I thought you were an engineer."

"My dear, have you not gone to see our marvelous Soo Locks?" The boarding house owner's facial features tugged in confusion. "Theo hasn't taken you?"

"No."

"Why, they're an engineering marvel!" Mrs. Elsner gestured to Theo to cut her a slice of cake, too.

"Do you enjoy your work, Garrett?" Theo passed the cake to his landlady.

"Well, it may not be as excitin' as building the Locks for those huge boats to go through, but I'd say I love my work." He wiped his face with his napkin. "Seein' something come alive out of the wood, that is an amazing feeling."

Theo smiled. "That's how I feel when I see the boats coming into and out of the locks. It is an engineering miracle and I get to be part of it."

Mrs. Elsner took a bite of the heavily frosted cake and then set her fork down. "And you, dear, do you enjoy running a business?"

"What?" Lilly and Garrett exchanged a glance before she stiffened and looked to Theo for explanation.

"Your shop," he offered before sipping his tea.

"Ya openin' up your Aunt Lillian's place as a shop?" Garrett frowned.

"I think there's some confusion." That head of steam Lilly had worked up earlier resurfaced. "We really need to talk."

The boarding house door chime rang. Mrs. Elsner rose and went to the door.

A strange expression came over Theo's face and his eyes seemed to glaze over as he peered past Lilly at Mrs. Elsner's retreating form. "No. Please not now," he muttered almost to himself.

"What's that?" Lilly's question was ignored as Theo hastily departed the table, a dumbstruck look on his face.

He joined Mrs. Elsner, whose soft words didn't carry down the hall.

"Wonder what that's all about?" Garrett shifted, beside her. "If you ain't eatin' that ham, I'd gladly take it."

Sighing, she held up the plate for him to spear the untouched ham slice with his fork.

"Mighty tasty. Better'n Rebecca's attempts at cookin' ham."

"You better not let her hear you say that." Lilly tried to give him a stern look, but he was too busy bent over his slab of ham, slicing it into chunks.

Exclamations rang out from the hallway. Lilly was tempted to turn around and look out the dining room's entryway and toward the front door.

"Mother!"

Lilly stiffened. Mrs. Elsner's comments made it clear that Theo was educated, which Lilly had figured, and from a prominent Detroit family, which she hadn't known. What was he doing skulking around looking for secondhand teacups for, then? And why did he tell those awful women that she sold tea sets?

When she returned, Mrs. Elsner wore a somber expression. She was followed by a dour-faced but elegantly attired woman whose nose wrinkled as though she smelled skunk.

"So this is where my son lives?" Her high nasal voice fit her narrow shrewish face.

Garrett stood and offered his hand, which the woman looked at until he dropped it. "Your son is gettin' a good feed bag on at this place, ma'am."

Her light eyes widened against her pale wrinkled skin. She glared at Theo, who appeared dumbstruck. "Who is this man?"

Her cousin's smile faltered. "He pointed to Lilly, this here is Lilly Smith, my cousin and I'm Garrett Christy, master craftsman for the Grand Hotel."

"Oh. . ." Was that fear on her face? Distress? Theo's mother reached out for him and she clutched his hand. "I'm a little dizzy."

Theo pulled back a chair for her, at the end of the table. "Mother, what's wrong?"

She waved him away. "I'll be fine. Your sister fouled up my tickets so I took things into my own hands."

The grandfather clock in the corner chimed eight times.

Mrs. Elsner cleared her throat as she took her seat. "I hate to bring this up, but with the hour so late I must tell you, Mrs. Reynolds that I have no extra rooms."

The matron blinked at her son. "Theo has a cottage rented for me, don't you dear?"

"I'm afraid I don't." His lower lip puckered up over his upper lip.

"He only received your daughter's letter today and your telegram, too." Mrs. Elsner rose from the table. "We'll leave you in privacy to discuss your plans."

Garrett's dark eyebrows drew together and he took Lilly's hand and squeezed it.

Lilly knew what Mama would have her do. "Your mother can stay with us. With me. My sisters aren't here yet."

What had she just gotten herself into?

Chapter 5

Dawn came early, accompanied by songbirds warbling outside Lilly's third story window. She yawned and stretched. With no maids nor any kind of servant, would Mrs. Reynolds expect to be waited on hand and foot? Theo's mother certainly let Garrett tote and carry for her the previous night.

Rising, Lilly nibbled her lower lip. Should she hire help? Just the thought unnerved her. Her, Lilly from the mountains of Kentucky and a log cabin that housed a family of seven when Pa was alive. But she had no sisters here to help her. She'd do it. She'd place an ad that day. And maybe she should get a handyman, too.

After getting washed and dressed, Lilly went downstairs and prepared breakfast for the three of them. She returned upstairs to the second floor, where Garrett was emerging from the bathroom, his face damp and hair slicked back.

"I've got breakfast ready." Lilly waved to him to follow her downstairs.

"Theo's ma is still snorin' up a storm in there."

Lilly would not make breakfast twice. But, the poor woman had traveled a long way the previous day. "Let's let her sleep."

Garrett followed her, both of them stepping carefully on the stair treads. "Let's get all caught up by our lonesome before she rises."

Soon, they'd gathered their breakfast of bacon, biscuits, cheesy eggs, and hot coffee with cream and carried it outside to the backyard.

"It's so lovely out here." Lilly sighed as she set down her plate on the wrought iron table top.

Garrett held her chair out for her. "Be a might prettier if you'd put somethin' between the garden and that there tool shed."

"That's what Theo said." Lilly adjusted her skirts around her as Garrett repositioned the heavy chair.

"Well, he's right smart, ain't he?" He laughed and then sat down across from her, where he'd set his plate.

She smiled at him. "Will you say the blessing?"

"Sure thing." He bowed his dark hair, a lock falling forward across his forehead. "Lord, Mrs. Reynolds has traveled a far distance and I can feel in my spirit that somethin' ain't right with her. But You know, Lord, and we ask you to help her."

Lilly lifted her head and peeked at her cousin, whose head was still bowed. She'd been too rattled by the woman's arrival to notice anything wrong with her. What did Garrett mean?

"And, Lord, we ask you to bless this food that You supplied. Give me travel safety home to my family and bless the children and the little one growin' inside her Lord. In Jesus's name, amen."

"Thank you." Lilly sipped her coffee. "I wonder what you mean about Theo's mother."

Garrett bit into his biscuit and chewed, gazing across at her with those dark eyes, so like Mama's. "I don't know if that lady is ill or if she's just given up hope."

How well she knew that feeling. With Mama dying and her sisters about to become her wards. Lilly had given up hope when the letter had come from Aunt Lillian's attorney. She folded her hands in her lap and looked down. Her hands may be chapped from cleaning but compared to the chipped nails and red rough hands, always seeming to attract dirt, constant when she dwelt in the mountains, they looked fine. What about her sisters? Were they hoping she'd hurry and get them up north, or was that Mama's hope?

"Lilly? You all right?"

"Hmm? Yes." Lilly met his gaze. "Just thinking about Mama and my sisters."

"They comin' soon?"

"I'm not sure." She inhaled the scent of lilacs, carried by the light breeze.

Garrett sipped his black coffee. "You said last night that your Ma was better."

"She is, but I think Daisy and Camellia got it in their heads that life might be better here."

"Awful cold in the winter." He pointed to the house. "But I think your cabin could fit in your new home maybe four times over."

"And more." What a blessing.

Stone crunched beneath someone's feet on the path on the side of the house.

"Lilly and Garrett?" Theo called out. "Are you there?"

The side gate opened and Theo entered the garden, pushing aside overgrown lilac bushes. "No one answered the door."

The right side of Garrett's mouth tugged upward. "The butler ain't in just yet."

"Ah." Theo, dressed in tan gabardine pants removed his brown wool slouch hat. "And I take it Mother is still asleep."

"Take a load off." Garrett gestured to the empty chair beside Lilly.

"Would you like breakfast?" Lilly made to rise but Theo raised his palm to stop her.

"Already ate at the boarding house. I'm here to help with that screen." He narrowed his eyes, gazing to the far back of the property where a faded cedar structure that looked ready for the woodpile stood.

Surely Garrett wasn't planning on taking on that venture. The rickety thing would make a good bonfire.

"I reckon I can stay and help ya." Garrett shoved a huge forkful of eggs into his mouth.

"There's wood stacked overhead in the shed." Theo jerked his thumb in that direction. "And also what looks like enough firewood to last a few months."

So much for chopping up what her neighbor called a *folly*, to burn. Why the irritable older man called it that, she didn't know. Seemed unkind. At one point that shelter must have been right pretty.

Theo rubbed the side of his handsome face. "I wish I knew more about fixing everyday items."

Garrett frowned. "You're an educated man fixin' up one of the wonders of our time. No shame in not knowin' about everything."

Instead of relaxing, Theo ran his hand repeatedly along his cheek.

What would it be like to touch his face? To stroke her fingers along his firm jawline? Would he lean in and kiss her?

"Lilly?"

"Hmm?" She blinked back at Theo.

"I said, I wonder if your aunt planned on doing something more with this garden."

"I have no idea." Lilly smiled at Theo as he sat beside her, his knee jostling her skirt.

The faint spicy scent of men's cologne and the tang of shaving soap mingled with the breakfast's aroma and garden's perfume. What a pleasant combination, but one that promised something that felt just beyond her reach. Longing welled up in her for something more from this man. A home. A future.

"You look deep in thought." Theo touched her shoulder lightly. "I hope Mother hasn't been too much trouble."

"No." She cupped her coffee mug in her hands, feeling somewhat traitorous at not drinking his favored drink of tea.

Garrett threw back a swig of coffee, finishing off his cup. "That was right good coffee. If only that was enough to cure what's ailing your mother."

Theo arched an eyebrow. "What do you mean?"

Lilly sighed. "Garrett thinks something is troubling her."

"Indeed." Theo glanced between the two of them. "Mother has her secrets to reveal in her own good time, but I can tell you she's not been the same since my father died."

"My mother lost the will to live." Lilly blinked back tears.

Theo took her hand in his. "I'm sorry."

"But ya said she's doin' fine now, right?" Garrett patted at his mouth with his napkin.

"She is." But maybe she wasn't telling the truth. Maybe she'd only partially recovered and was trying to ease Lilly's mind. Maybe she was sending eighteen-year-old Delphinium and sixteen-year-old Camellia up to be sure the other girls would be fine. Maybe she was planning on sending the youngest to Aunt Jessamine.

"She asked my father if he could take the two younger ones, if she. . ." Garrett pushed back from the table and stood.

"She did?"

"Yup."

"When was that?" Her gut tightened.

Both she and Theo looked up at her cousin. He scratched his chin. "Musta been right before ya got up here."

She exhaled a whoosh of relief and Theo leaned in to kiss her cheek. A thrill shot through her at the warmth of his lips on her face, brief though the contact was.

"Ya gotta give your Ma a reason for hope, you two." He winked at them. "Plannin' for a wedding might take her mind offa things."

Lilly gasped but Theo only laughed.

Her cheeks grew hot and she rose from the table, Theo following her.

Theo stretched. "Mother nearly exhausted herself planning my sisters' weddings in the last few years."

"There," Lilly glared at Garrett and waved her hand toward Theo, "you have it. She'd not be buoyed up by planning a wedding."

"The planning wasn't the only problem. Mother and Father constantly quarreled over the budget. . ." Theo's countenance drooped.

"A preacher, a license, and a couple of witnesses don't cost much." Garrett tugged at his suspenders. "And if the church ladies throw you a banquet, that's free."

Once again, Lilly shot her older cousin what she hoped was a silencing glare. He just laughed as he turned and headed off toward the shed.

Theo squeezed her hand and released it. "That's one happily married man, I believe."

"I believe you're right."

"He just wants everyone to be as happy as he is." Theo took her hand and raised it to his lips, pressing a kiss that seared through her. "Please don't feel pressured by his words."

"I don't." She wanted him to kiss her hand again. To kiss her cheek. Her lips. Her own heart pressured her -- not her cousin's words.

Theo looked up toward the second floor of the house. "Will we bother her with sawing and hammering?"

Birds erupted in song, some robins chasing each other between the tall spruce trees that bordered the garden. "If she can sleep through all their chatter then I imagine it won't bother her, but let me go up and check on her."

"Thanks." Once again he stepped close to her, this time pressing a warm kiss to her forehead. If she tipped her chin up, would he kiss her lips? She dare not be so forward, even though she wanted to.

She was falling in love with this man. Not that she knew what that felt like but if thinking about someone all the time and wanting them with you and wanting the best for them, then she was.

Lilly picked up the dirty dishes and carried them inside. She'd wash them after she checked on Mrs. Reynolds.

Upstairs, the air was still and stuffy. She needed to open the windows and finish dusting and cleaning the last bedroom on this floor. Lilly knocked on the door. No answer. She tried again. Finally she cracked the door open and peeked in. Sunlight, around the edges of the blinds, gave slight illumination through the curtains. Lilly allowed her eyes to adjust and opened the door fully. The woman didn't move beneath the covers. Lilly returned to the hall and located a kerosene lamp, which she'd use to supplement the low gaslight. She lit the wick, placed the glass cover back on, and returned to the room.

Drawing near the bedside, she held the lamp high. Theo's mother was flushed and perspiration trickled down her face despite the cool room. Lilly set the lamp on the nightstand and pressed her hand to the woman's forehead. She was burning up.

"Oh Lord, please have mercy." She touched the woman's shoulder.

Theo's mother moaned. "Water." Her eyes fluttered open. "Water."

Lilly removed the glass from the bedside carafe and poured water into it. "Can you sit up?"

Mrs. Reynolds struggled to lift her head but then let it flop back onto the pillow. "Please. . .water."

Heart hammering in her chest, Lilly placed a hand beneath the woman's head, covered with a satin bonnet of some type. She raised her up enough to take some sips of water.

"I'm going to send for the doctor." Not that she knew where a doctor could be found.

"More. . . water."

This time, Lilly removed the satin bonnet. "This might be making things worse. Holding the heat in from your fever."

With her eyes closed, Mrs. Reynolds tried to lift her head, without success.

Lilly tossed the head covering aside and once again helped the woman to drink. "I'm going to get Theo to fetch the doctor. I'll be back in a minute."

"Stay. . ."

"After I send for the doctor."

Lilly ran down the stairs and through the back. She found Theo and Garrett sawing boards. "Your mother is very ill. She needs a doctor right away."

"What?" Theo stopped and set his saw aside.

"She has a bad fever."

"Let me check on her."

"Didn't you hear me?" Lilly shook her index finger at him. "She's burning up and can barely lift her head."

When he glanced up at the room, she poked him.

"Go for the doctor now."

"All right." Theo blinked as though her words were finally sinking in. "There's one just two blocks down. I'll run over."

Garrett set his saw down and wiped his hands on a rag. "Anything I can do?"

"Pray."

He took her hands, and they bent their heads as he uttered a heartfelt prayer. When he added prayers for her mother, too, tears flowed from Lilly's eyes. Dear God please let both our mothers be well.

Several hours later, the three of them gathered on the front porch, teacups in hand, Lilly rocking and the two men staring out over the yard. The doctor had come again, after checking Mrs. Reynolds in the morning and was upstairs.

Theo grasped a rosebud from one of the teacups she'd tried to organize that day. He twirled between his index fingers. "I'm sorry, Lilly, for drawing you into this."

"It's all right." Gentle breezes rippled the leaves of the young maple tree and the lilac bushes.

Garrett eyed the two of them. "Seems the good Lord put you two together for a purpose." The dainty teacup in the former lumberjack's big hands looked absurd as he raised it to his lips.

Theo lifted his chin and looked overhead toward the cloud-dotted robin's egg blue skies, as though he could see God there. "I don't like imposing on others."

"It's all right." Lilly sipped the strong black tea, flavored with honey.

"But you'll not be able to conduct business if you're tending to my mother and we've already interrupted your visit with your cousin."

Garrett exchanged a glance with Lilly. "What business?"

She rolled her eyes upward. "Theo thinks I have a tea shop."

"That would be my wife who owns a tea shop, not Lilly." Garrett pointed to two huge crates on the end of the porch. "I'm taking all those teacups and saucers back to Mackinac Island with me."

Theo's forehead crinkled and he gestured toward the house. "What is this place then?"

Exasperated, Lilly set her teacup in its saucer with a clatter. "Your mama is upstairs possibly ill to near death and you want to talk about my so-called business?"

Theo's cheeks flushed.

Garrett threw back the rest of his tea. "Soon as I hear what the doc says, I'll need to head out."

Steps sounded in descent on the interior staircase. Theo rose. "I hope he has good news."

Lilly waited, rocking.

The portly man opened the screen door and joined them, the slight breeze from the water ruffling the wispy gray hair that framed his solemn face. "I wish I could put her in the hospital."

"Should you?" Theo ran his hand over his jawline.

"I don't want to move her. I fear she'll worsen."

Garrett stood. "Is there a private nurse available, doc?"

"None."

"I'll do it." Lilly stopped rocking. "I took care of my Ma all this past year."

The doctor's gray eyes fastened on her. "And is she well now?"

"I. . ." She hoped so, but wasn't sure. Lilly looked away.

"Never mind, as long as you can tend her now — that's what matters."

Chapter 6

Lilly swept the porch so vigorously, she feared a layer of floor paint might be removed. She stopped and dragged her muslin-clad arm across her damp forehead. Street cleaners passed by, the young man in front brushing up the manure and the one behind him spraying water from a tank inside the wagon he pulled. She stopped to watch the two. It wouldn't be long until street traffic would pick up and Portage would be dotted with manure. But for now, for this early dawn moment, the avenue was clean. Wasn't sin like that? You asked God to forgive you and before you knew it, you'd sinned again.

She set aside her broom and sank into the rocking chair.

"Excuse me!" A voice called out as someone grabbed Lilly's arm, waking her.

She must have fallen asleep. Lilly threw off the arm, startled by the stranger's voice and tried to rise, but fell back into the rocking chair. Lilly opened her eyes to see a silver-haired woman, whose crinkled face bespoke her many years. An old-fashioned rolled brim black wool hat was pinned atop her tightly upswept hair.

Please Lord, not another person here thinking Lilly sold teacups. "Hello."

"Sorry to wake you, dearie, but I've got to get back to my shop before it opens."

Lilly blinked up at her. Finally, she positioned her legs and rose from the rocker. She towered over the petite woman, who now took two steps back. "My name is Lilly Smith. What is yours?"

The woman's thin lips parted. "Lillian's great-niece?"

"Yes, ma'am."

"Oh, my. I always feared it would come to this."

Lilly had worked herself to a frazzle the previous day and hadn't slept much because of Mrs. Reynolds being so ill. Obviously this stranger hadn't come to pay her respects, although a dozen or so had greeted Lilly at church and had done so. "What is your business with me, ma'am?" My, her voice sounded snappish!

"Well. . .I." The tiny woman squared her shoulders, causing the thick shiny fabric to strain. "I always thought Lillian just might start up her own tea shop, with all the collection she acquired."

Help me have patience, Lord. Lilly turned her head toward the door, straining to hear if Mrs. Reynolds needed anything. "Auntie sure didn't need all that stuff for one person."

"No. But now you've put it to good use, haven't you?"

"Ma'am, you haven't even given me your name and you're asking all kinds of personal questions." Lilly's patience had grown thin despite her prayer. If this old gal had walked up on their property and started in on her mother like this, Mama would have grabbed the broom and ran her off right quick.

A faint cry sounded through the screen door, "Lilly? Can you help?"

"Excuse me, but I'm needed."

"You're not going to get away with this!" The stranger called after her.

Lilly turned to face her. Maybe the woman was deranged. They had a few of those folks in the hollows of the mountains. But this lady looked too finely put together. "Ma'am, I may not be a real nurse but I can take care of Mrs. Reynolds just fine. So if you're not here about the nursing position then scat!"

"Well! I never!"

Lilly went inside, pulled the screen closed and secured the hook, then slammed the big oak door with gusto. Tears welled up in her eyes. Maybe she should go back home where folks were more civil to one another. She needed her sisters and her Ma.

"Lilly!" Theo's mother's faint voice called from her room.

"Coming!" She lifted her skirts and ran up the stairs, glancing out the window as she rounded the landing. The stranger stood on the sidewalk, speaking with a police officer and pointing to the house.

There couldn't possibly be a law against nursing a sick woman in one's own home. Was there?

"Theo?" His boss's voice was accompanied by a puff of smoke blown upward toward the paneled ceiling.

"Yes, sir?" He tried to focus on the diagrams spread out before him. He needed to get telegrams to his sisters to explain that their mother hadn't improved, despite the physician's best measures.

"You seem distracted." His gaze traveled around the table, touching briefly on each of the other engineers.

He needed this job. Now more than ever. Doctor bills were adding up. When Mother recovered, he didn't want her traveling any time soon. Thank God Lilly had kept her at her aunt's house, otherwise Theo's savings would be shot, as well as his dream that one day. . .

"Theo?"

"Yes?"

"I'm taking you off this project."

The blood seemed to rush from his head, as dizziness shook him. "No. I'm fine."

"Go home. Go look after your mother."

His vision, momentarily blurred, cleared. He'd not said anything to his supervisor about his mother's illness.

"I read it in this morning's society column." Mr. Dickerson cleared his throat. "The ladies are all atwitter that Mrs. Reynolds has arrived, but concerned over her illness."

Theo's mouth dropped open but he couldn't manage any words. He clamped his lips tightly together.

Mr. Dickerson waved him away. "Go tend to her and we'll see you back later this afternoon."

"Yes, sir. Thank you." Theo rose and nodded toward him and then toward his colleagues, who all wore a concerned expression.

As he got his belongings and left the building, his peer's faces clung in his memory, sending a chill through him. Their apprehensive faces sent more distress through him than any of the doctor's pronouncements.

Dear God, I need help. We need healing for my Mother. Don't take her. Help me, Lord. Help us – all of us, and bless Lilly for being so good to us, dear Father.

Swiping away moisture from his eyes, Theo exited the building and soon strode through the park-like canopy of trees bordering the property. Birdsong called out in exultation, all manner of chirps and songs, and a mocking bird imitated the sound of a fire wagon's gong. He couldn't help but smile, hearing it. Beneath his feet, thick grass dotted with clover, gave way as he strode on. Bees buzzed around rose bushes that clumped here and there. As he reached the edge, a border of hydrangea bushes, covered in blooms of white and blue, greeted him with delicate fragrance. Nearby, a solitary poppy bloomed bright and vibrant against the carpet of green grass. One bloom, surrounded by what eventually would be more orange-red blossoms. All alone. Like Lilly. And beautiful and different like her.

When they married, and had a family, she'd be surrounded by children. His cheeks heated at the thought of producing those babies. They could fill up a house full. Perhaps he'd better court her first.

He strode toward the house when a livery carriage pulled down the driveway alongside Lily's house. A little girl leaned out the window. "Ma, look how big it is!"

Theo stopped and watched. Was she taking in boarders? What about his mother? Would she need to be moved? Lilly hadn't said a thing. He resumed walking toward the house.

One after another, stairstep girls stepped out of the carriage, followed by a thin haggard woman, whose wispy hair escaped her horror of a hat. Their faded calico dresses and scuffed brown boots reminded him of someone else.

Should he greet them? Should he run into the house and get Lilly and check on his mother? He drew in a deep breath, before striding toward the arrivals. "Good day, are you here for Miss Smith?"

"Miss Smith? Don't that sound proper, Ma?" The tallest of the four girls, with ebony curls frizzing about her pale face, giggled.

"Hush now!" The mother frowned at her daughter before staring up at Theo with the same eyes as Lilly.

"Mrs. Smith?" Theo croaked as he held out his hand, intending to bow over this woman's hand and kiss it, as he'd been taught.

The woman clutched her hand to her midriff. "Yes? Who are you?"

"I'm Lilly's. . ." Her future husband? He'd not even asked the question much less told her he loved her nor even courted her properly. "I'm her friend."

"Friend is it?" Her lips pursed. "Looks like we got here just in time. No decent man comes calling during daytime. Are you some kind of no account?"

A no account? A phrase he'd not heard, but surely pejorative. "No, madam. My mother is ill and I've come to check on her."

The woman gathered her girls around like chicks. "What would your mother be doing here at my Lilly's home?"

The front door opened. "Ma!" The screen door slammed behind Lilly as she flew toward them, tears streaming down her cheeks.

Theo used that opportunity to slip away into the house, his heart hammering. He'd check on his mother and then that afternoon, he'd beg the doctor to make room for her at the hospital, no matter if his "no account" at the bank was drained. He hurried upstairs, and rapped at his mother's door.

No answer. He knocked again before gently opening the door. Despite the sun streaming through the windows, curtains parted, Mother lay sleeping, her hair arranged around her on her pillow. On the washstand, a wet cloth perched perilously from the basin's edge, water dripping onto the wood. He went to the stand and placed the rag into the water then lifted the bowl. He'd dump it, to spare Lilly the trouble, and then return to grab the pitcher and refill it. Growing up, he'd never have thought of such simple things. Servants slipped into and out of rooms so unobtrusively he and his family members didn't realize they'd come and gone. How spoiled he'd been. At the rooming house, Mrs. Elsner no doubt did the same for him. All he and the other boarders had been required to do was to leave their bed linens at the foot of their beds on wash day, when she took the laundry to the cleaners. During the week when the cleaners had closed, Mrs. Elsner had washed everything in her newfangled wringer washer, in the back washhouse. Did Lilly's aunt own one? Who was doing all the linen?

He had to do something to help.

Lilly pressed a teacup into Theo's hand, and the warmth of her fingers sent a thrill through him. He leaned forward. Her eyes widened slightly, as they stood on the landing outside his mother's room.

"Lilly!" Iris, the second youngest of the four flower-named girls hollered up the stairwell before tromping upstairs.

Theo backed up.

A pretty pink tinged Lilly's high cheekbones. "What do u want Iris?"

"It's been three whole days and you haven't taken us to the lake, like you and Theo promised."

Theo tweaked the girl's nose. "Let me check on my mother and then we'll see."

Lilly held her index finger to her pretty lips. "Shhh! Listen!"

From inside his mother's room, she and Lilly's mother laughed uproariously.

"Is that so?" Mother's voice was as strong as ever.

"Sure as shootin', I'm tellin' ya, that Irishman musta sold over a dozen cases of this elixir but I was his miracle case!"

Lilly rolled her eyes. "She's still talking about that snake oil salesman."

"He weren't selling snake oil. It was medicine." The young girl frowned up at her sister.

"Oh, botheration. The only thing he sold Ma was hope."

"Hope?"

Inside Mother laughed. "What a shame Dr. Fischer isn't here to see another of his miracle cases."

Lilly leaned in toward him and Iris. "I smelled that bottle. All it has in it is vanilla, sassafras, brandy, and I think some crushed rosemary."

Theo stifled a laugh.

Iris glared up at him. "That potion cured my Ma and you shouldn't laugh, Mister."

He tweaked her nose again. "Call me Theo, and since I'm the one driving you to the lake, I think you'd better rid yourself of that grumpy face."

From within the room, another gale of laughter pealed loudly. Lilly opened the door. "Everything all right in here?"

Theo ducked around her and could see his mother wiping away tears of laughter from her eyes.

"I haven't had so much fun since I was a girl and away at boarding school. Did I ever tell you about that, Theo?"

His mother had been shunned by many of the other girls and her best friend had been one of the maids. They'd get together in secret, play cards, and engage in Mother's favorite thing – having their very own tea party. "Yes, Mother, you did."

"I sure miss Amanda."

Mrs. Smith patted Mother's hand. "You should send her a note. I'll even write it for you. Me and all my girls were educated right there in the valley. The oldest three went all the way through eighth grade."

Mother's features tugged in an obvious attempt to prevent her disapproval.

"Do you have her address?" Mrs. Smith was as persistent as her daughter.

Theo almost interrupted to reply that of course his mother hadn't kept up with one of the school servants.

"Oh, yes, I do. It's in my valise."

Mother seemed full of surprises today.

"Is that what you call that bag yonder?" Lily's mother ducked her head in that direction.

"Yes. I have a small address book in there."

"Vall-eese." Mrs. Smith rose and went to where the bag sat in a corner. "Ain't that a fancy name?"

"Ma?" Lily wrapped an arm around her sister. "We'd like to take the girls to the park for a little picnic."

Her mother ducked her chin. "We're fine, ain't we, Mrs. Reynolds?"

"Indeed. Go on. Just bring us up our tea before you go, would you, Lilly, dear?"

Lilly nodded before she practically sprinted from the room, leaving Theo with Iris.

Theo rocked in his broughams for a moment. "Anything else we can get you, Mother, before we leave?"

"Yes, we want a card table brought up, along with four decks of cards, please."

Mrs. Smith clapped her hands together. "And pennies, too."

"Pennies?" Mother arched a brow.

Lilly's mother shrugged. "In case we place a wager."

"I see."

"Lilly gave me a bag of nickels." Grinning, Mrs. Smith displayed a small muslin bag. "It's for the girls – when they want to run for a treat."

"Too many sweets aren't good for children," Mother sniffed.

"Well, we can use these if ya want to bet bigger than a penny."

"No, thank you. A good old copperhead will suffice."

Iris peered up at Theo. "What's a snake got to do with anything and how does that stuff ice?"

"I'll explain later." He squeezed her shoulder. "Go get the girls and tell them we'll be leaving in about twenty minutes."

What a change to be the older and not the younger one in these exchanges. His sisters had spoiled him, but they'd also teased Theo unmercifully and loved to boss him around.

"Sure thing, Theo." She beamed up at him. "I like that name. Theo sounds better than Mister."

"It sure does." He mussed her hair. "Go on now or we'll be late."

Mother waved him over to the bed. "We'd like some ice cream later, if you can get it. Daisy told me earlier that she saw a sign near the train depot."

"I believe you're much better, Mother." Already asking favors and ordering people around.

"I am." She and Mrs. Smith exchanged a knowing glance.

"Now you git along there, Theo, while I tell your ma all about how handsome that Irishman was who made that potion what cured her and me."

"Yes, ma'am. I'll get that folding table and bring it right back." Theo headed out the door as Lilly was wheeling in a tea cart that reminded him of one from their country home. "She'll love this."

"The tea should be ready in a few minutes." She pointed to the cookies and biscuits on two china plates. "This should hold them until we get back. I'll get my shawl in case there is a chill, and my hat. Then I'll bring the tea up."

Twin rosebud teacups and saucers dominated the cart. Silver spoons were set to the side, atop pink linen napkins. Matching plates held the food. A space at the center was presumably where the teapot would sit.

"Do you have a card table?"

"In the parlor. And would you pour the water over the tea while you are down there?" She smiled up at him, her face so close, he could bend and kiss her, if only. . . "It would save me time."

He swallowed and straightened. "I'd be happy to."

"Don't they look precious together?" Mother's intoned statement startled him. Had she really just given her blessing?"

"They sure do." Mrs. Smith's eyes widened as she surveyed the tea cart. "Just like those there cups go perfect with them saucers."

Chapter 7

Dressed in their swimming clothes, the oldest two of Lilly's younger sisters strode out to the Lake Superior shoreline, Delphinium twirling her parasol. When she bumped it into Camellia, the younger sister yelped. Lilly smoothed out the skirt of her navy and white swimming dress, and then took Theo's hand.

Her two youngest sisters, Daisy and Iris, ran ahead of Lilly and Theo and then stopped to unroll their plaid basket near a family with several children near their ages.

When both Camellia and Delphinium took to twirling their parasols, attracting male attention, Lilly scowled at Theo. "We best go in with them."

He swung his free hand up to cover his chuckle.

"What's so funny?" She pulled him forward. "Come on."

He laughed as they hurried to catch up with the young women. As they passed he called to Daisy and Iris, "Sit tight! We'll be right back."

Lilly huffed. "We won't be right back if we go in with them."

Again he chuckled. "You needn't worry about them going in too far."

"Why not?" She narrowed her gaze at him as they passed by a family of picnickers seated on a quilt, a wicker basket overflowing with cherries, sandwiches wrapped in paper, a box of crackers, and a large jar of tea. "My sisters can't swim."

"Shouldn't be an issue." Ducking his head, he ran his thumb over his lower lip.

"Why not?" As they drew up closer to the flouncing young ladies, Lilly shook her head. These were the first new clothes in a long while for pretty auburn-haired Camellia and dark-haired Delphinium. These were also the only genuinely frilly and feminine garb they'd ever had.

Theo pointed to the blue-gray water, which rippled beneath a bright blue sky dotted with puffy clouds. "You'll soon see."

"Theo! I really don't want to sit here and watch my sisters drown!" She strode faster toward the girls, Theo keeping up with her.

They'd almost closed in on them when two young dandies popped up from their blankets. One bowed toward Camellia and the other toward dark-eyed Delphinium. Lilly blew out a breath of exasperation. Her sisters were too young for beaus. Weren't they? She chewed her lower lip.

Theo squeezed her hand. "I know those two fellows from work. They're skirt-chasers."

Lilly released his hand. "Well, do something then."

"If you'll give me just a minute, I won't have the necessity."

"What? You need to use the necessary right now?" She glanced around, not spying an outhouse. "When my sisters are being bothered by those men?"

He chuckled and wrapped an arm around her shoulder. "No, just watch."

Theo certainly did seem relaxed. With him so close to her, Lilly's heartbeat kicked up a notch. Or maybe it was because she was worried about her sisters. Theo turned her toward him, and looked down at her with such adoration, that she could scarcely catch her breath. He leaned in closer. Theo was choosing this time to bestow their first kiss? She stiffened, just as he quickly kissed the top of her head and then turned her once more toward the sandy beach.

Her sisters, flanked by each of the young men, tentatively crossed the sand, holding their shoes in their hands. Despite the unusually warm, early June day, none of the children in the families were down by the water. In fact, as Lilly broke away from Theo and ran toward the little group, she saw that no one else was going in. In the distance, ships sailed toward the Soo Locks, which she'd finally gotten to see on their trip out.

She approached the shoreline. A few children skipped stones on the water, calling out the number they'd skipped over the waves.

As Camellia and Delphinium stepped into the water, a collective shriek went up. "It's cold!"

"This here water is freezing!" Her brown-eyed sister shot one of the young men a scathing look before she ran straight back to Lilly and Theo, who had now joined her.

Still at the shore, the two young bucks laughed and patted each other on the back.

"Why didn't you tell us?" Camellia demanded of Theo.

His cheeks flushed and he ducked his chin. "I guess I should have."

"You guess?" Her sister harrumphed. "It's like ice water in there!"

A wicked gleam lit Camellia's green eyes. "I guess the Smith girls will have to help you get an early bath then."

Lilly watched as the four girls pulled, pushed and prodded Theo down to the lake, and he good-naturedly allowed them to push him in. Life with him would be grand. Life with him? Since when had that been an option? God had brought her to this place to give her, and her family, a new life. Was Theo part of that?

As all three of them ran back toward her, the clusters of families on the beach called out, cheered, clapped and whistled.

Theo rushed at her and clasped her in his cold dripping arms. He lifted Lilly up and twirled her around. Dizzy, when he finally set her down, she clung to him, despite the chilling wetness that soaked through her own swimming garb. He pressed his lips close to her ear. "After I put up with that dunking, I think you owe me something."

"What?" She shook, but it had nothing to do with the lake water soaking her and everything to do with his words.

He kissed her cheek. "After I ask your mother, then I'll let you know what adequate recompense is."

Lilly wasn't sure what that meant but she'd ask on the way home. After rejoining Iris and Daisy, they had their picnic. Afterward, they strolled around the park, then loaded back up into the carriage.

They arrived back in town well before dark, which was late-coming in the Upper Peninsula's summers, Lilly had learned. At Aunt Lil's house, they'd had to add extra blinds to the west-facing rooms. The sun sometimes didn't set until after nine and the sky was not dark until after ten. As Theo directed the horses up Portage Avenue, Lilly spied movement near the house.

"Oh, no." Lilly pressed a hand to her mouth. "It's that awful woman again."

"Who? I see a policeman up there, but. . ."

"A policeman?" Fourteen-year-old Iris, in the back seat, leaned up behind Lilly, tossing her dark-blond braid over her shoulder. "Did your Ma do something bad, Theo?"

He gave the reins a flick and the horses picked up their pace. He pulled into the drive alongside the porch, where Ma was talking with the stranger and the policeman. When Theo set the brake, Lilly quickly jumped down, trailed by her sisters like a flock of chicks.

"What's going on here?" Lilly narrowed her eyes at the strange lady before turning to address the policeman. "This lady is trespassing on my property."

Mama crossed her arms and nodded her head. "That's just what I told her. And when I offered to give her a broom-escort down the walk, she refused it."

"Well, I never!" The silver-haired lady tapped at the officer's shoulder with her index finger. "Do I have to take this kind of maltreatment?"

The policeman raised both hands. "Everyone settle down here. I'm sure this is just a misunderstanding."

"There's no misunderstanding. Lillian collected teacups for years, intending to put me out of business and now this upstart is operating a business without a license!"

"What?" Lilly gasped and looked up at Theo, for him to clarify, but he said nothing.

Mama picked up the broom. "She needs to be put in that new asylum in Newberry."

"Why, I never!"

"We're all guests here, lady. Do you know what that is?" Mama scowled so fiercely she could peel the skin off a tater. "It's what you ain't. You ain't a guest – you're a trespasser."

Behind Mama, the screen door opened. "What's going on down here?"

"Mother, go back to bed." Theo moved past the others, excusing himself as he went.

"See here, I'm Samantha Reynolds, a guest here, recovering from an illness and this young lady has been nothing but kind to me." Theo's mother pressed a hand against the door jamb. "Of what crime are you accusing her?"

"Yeah?" Iris muttered, rolling her blue-green eyes.

The officer patted his baton. Was he thinking of using it? Lilly cringed. "Everybody settle down now."

"That's right, ma'am." The policeman turned toward Lilly. "Are you operating a tea shop from this home, Miss Smith?"

"No!"

"Of course not," Mrs. Reynolds and Ma echoed.

Theo assumed a sheepish posture. "Aren't you, Lilly?"

"No." She stared at him. "Whatever gave you that idea?" She should have corrected him long ago. But she'd thought he must realize she wasn't.

"See!" The tiny woman jabbed at the officer again. "She's selling goods."

"Do you have any proof?" The blond-haired policemen tapped his foot.

Theo rubbed his chin and avoided eye contact.

Lilly sighed and met the tea shop owner's gaze. "Ma'am, you and Mr. Reynolds obviously are confused. I did allow him to have some of Aunt Lillian's teacups and saucers, for his mother and he insisted on paying."

"There, she said it!" The shopkeeper jabbed at the air with her index finger.

"But I had him put the money in a jar up there on the porch." Lilly pointed to where it sat.

Theo picked up the jar and lifted its lid.

"It's empty, though."

"That's called making a sales transaction and it is illegal. *Illegal* young lady! It might be different down South where you live but up here. . ."

Lilly cut off the tirade with a wave of her hand. "That's because I took the money and donated it at church last week."

"Where?" the woman demanded.

"St. Mary's. My aunt was a member there."

"I'm a member, and I never saw you go up." The lady huffed.

"That's because I met with the priest privately and gave the donation in my Aunt Lillian's name, along with another amount she'd specified."

The policeman nodded. "That's easy enough to verify, with your permission, miss."

"Certainly."

Mama uncrossed her arms and gathered up the girls. "Come on, let's get you out of them silly swimming dresses and into bed."

"Goodnight, son!" Mrs. Reynolds waved to Theo. She went inside with Mama and Lilly's sisters, as the police officer and tea shop proprietress left, too.

Lilly strode up the steps to her rocking chair and sat down. "Theo, you nearly had me arrested."

He held up both hands. "I didn't know what to say."

Suddenly tired, she closed her eyes. "I just need some time to myself."

"Forgive me, Lilly, I didn't realize exactly what your situation was."

It isn't his fault.

"Let me bid you goodnight then."

As he turned to walk away, she called out, "Wait. I'm sorry. If I were honest with myself, the truth is I didn't tell you early on because I'd hoped. . ."

Theo turned and faced her in the twilight night, fireflies glowing as they signaled one another. "Yes?"

"I'd hoped you'd keep coming in to buy more teacups for your mother." And now the whole household had been upset.

Laughter pealed from upstairs. Lilly lifted her chin.

Theo chuckled. "They're getting a kick out of what happened – at our expense."

She gave a short laugh. "Seems so."

"I don't think any harm has been done, save to the tea shop owner's pride."

"And I will make that up to her. Whether she accepts my apology, and my cherry pie, will be up to her."

"I'll take the pie if she doesn't." Theo took two steps closer, bent, and leaned his forehead against hers.

A thrill shot through her down to her toes as he pulled her up from the chair then drew her closer. He released her hands and wrapped his arms around her, pressing her against his broad chest. There, in the near-dark, they could have been the only two people in the world, despite the laughter continuing upstairs.

"Lilly, do you want to know what I wanted to ask your mother?"

Wrapped in his embrace, she didn't care. "Hmmm?"

"If she'd agree for me to court you."

Her shoulders briefly stiffened before she relaxed back into his arms, inhaling his spicy scent. "What do you think she'll say, especially since you're out here holding me in your arms?"

"Probably to ask you, since she isn't the one who'd have to put up with me."

Lilly laughed and pulled back to look up at him. Overhead, hundreds of stars began to appear as the skies went dark. The pressure of his warm fingers against her waist sent a shiver of anticipation through her. A passage from the *Song of Solomon* came to mind, one that admonished *"Daughters. . .do not stir love until it is the right time."* She might not have the verse right, but she understood its meaning.

"How about I ask what your cousin, Garrett, said to ask you?"

Drawing in a deep breath, prickles moved up and down her arms and back. Surely he hadn't. . .

"Will you marry me, Lilly?" Theo's husky voice resonated through her.

"Yes," she whispered. "But I think you've got the courting and askin' to marry thing all mixed up."

"Could be." His breath tickled her ear.

They stood, embracing one another, as the bullfrog began their nightly ribbitting.

"May I kiss you?"

She'd been waiting so long for this moment. Her first real kiss. What should she do? She stiffened and tilted her head back, eyes closed.

Theo laughed gently. "You seem pretty tense, Lilly."

"I'm not. I'm just waiting."

"Your back is stiff as a board." Theo ran his hands up and down the ruffled back of her swimming gown.

Shivers coursed through her. It was really happening. This man she'd grown to love was going to kiss her. Lilly leaned into Theo as his warm mouth covered hers. His lips were every bit as sweet as she'd imagined when she'd dreamed of him embracing her. He drew away then kissed her again, this time pressing a hand to the back of her head. He coaxed her even closer, running his other hand along her back. He kissed her cheek and then her neck, planting warm kisses as she sighed in contentment. She felt his arms shake as he kissed her ear and then pulled free just as she was wanting more. So much more.

He took her hands in his and drew them together. "Lilly, I must stop. I fear I've already taken too many liberties."

She tugged at his hands, wishing and willing for him to keep on kissing her. "I. . ."

The screen door opened and then slammed shut. "Thought that's what was goin' on down here." Mama's voice, though firm, held a bit of humor.

"Would a month from now be too soon?" Theo whispered.

"Mama," Lilly called out. "Mr. Reynolds wants to court me."

"But first I'd like to marry her!" Theo kissed the top of Lilly's head.

"City folk," Mama muttered. "Lilly will be locked in this so-called Tea Shoppe until ya come back with a marriage license, Mr. Reynolds."

Lilly pulled Theo's head closer to hers, again, and kissed his cheek. Then she whispered in his ear, "Be glad she's not got Pa's shotgun with her."

Theo laughed. "I'd get to marry you even sooner then."

Epilogue

Lilly's three youngest sisters, dressed in pastel hues, sat in the front right aisle of the Saint James Episcopal Church, where Theo was a member. Mama dabbed at her eyes. All of her Christy cousins with their wives and children and her uncle and his wife sat behind them. Lilly's own eyes began to fill. On the left, Theo's mother sat and his friends from church. His sisters had been unable to attend, but sent well wishes and some lovely wedding gifts.

Garrett took Lilly's arm. "You ready for this?"

"Seein' as Mama really meant it about keeping me cooped up until the wedding, I'd say so."

"I think she might be like my Pa and was punnin' you." He winked at her.

"I think you mean funning me, but she and Theo's mother kept me occupied, and us supervised, ever since the engagement."

Her cousin rubbed his chin. "Pa and I placed a wager with my sister, Jo, that your Ma meant Locked In, like the Soo Locks being right there yonder from your house.

Lilly gave a short laugh. "How much did you lose?"

"Pa and I won and split the winnings."

"What?!"

Wedding attendees swiveled to look toward the narthex.

Lilly squeezed Garrett's muscular arm. "So Theo and I could have seen each other more and been alone some, instead of surrounded by my sisters all the time?"

He laughed. "That's about the size of it."

"We could have snuck in some kisses in that new gazebo you made for our wedding gift!"

"Now, little cousin, that would have been a folly and you know it."

Before she could protest, organ music began and all the guests rose. Garrett marched her forward, beaming. He turned to wink at his wife and children as they passed by. When they reached Mama, she and Daisy, Iris, and Camellia were all wiping their eyes.

At the front stood Delphinium, attired in a lilac gown bedecked with as much lace and ribbon as could cover every square inch of the bodice. Opposite her, Theo's best man, Franz Klassen, shifted nervously. Was he reliving his own wedding?

Theo stood tall, his demeanor calm, hands clasped before him. Only the twitch of his dark eyebrows betrayed any anxiety. Lilly stifled a giggle. This was really happening. She was getting married.

At the altar, bouquets of roses and ferns, added their scent to her bouquet of mixed lilies tied off with a wide mauve satin ribbon. Theo had a single white calla lily tucked into his lapel. He'd never looked more handsome. The way he stared at her as she drew closer, eyes wide, made Lilly feel that all the hours of fittings for the wedding gown had been worthwhile. She'd never felt more lovely nor more cherished.

He mouthed, "I love you," at her and she beamed back at him.

Hope flooded her. Hope for a future with this man she loved. Hope she'd almost lost only a few months earlier.

Thank you, God, for everything.

Sun shone through the new stained glass windows, as though the Lord was acknowledging her silent prayer of thanks. There was so much to be grateful for, and this was only the beginning of her new life.

Before she knew it, they'd said their vows and somehow Theo had placed his grandmother's ornate gold band upon her ring finger. She was Mrs. Theodore Reynolds now! Everything passed in a blur as they exited the church, the onlookers beaming in approval.

Outside, Theo drew her into a quick, but sound, kiss—one that promised many more to come. He pulled her close to his vested chest, and she could hear his heart pounding. Hers was galloping just as fast. How she loved him. Her husband. Theo slackened his hold and bent to kiss her, again. She was beginning to forget where they were when someone cleared his throat.

"Now hold on there, you two!" Garrett's deep voice was followed by a chuckle as he escorted Mama outside.

Lilly's cousin, Richard Christy, a giant of a man, escorted Theo's mother into the sunshine, as they all formed a receiving line to accept congratulations.

Mrs. Reynolds craned her neck back to look up at Richard. "Thank you for helping your brother build that wonderful gazebo for Theo and Lilly."

Theo's brows furrowed and his lower lip puckered out. "It reminds me of great-grandmother's folly."

Lilly whacked him playfully on the arm. "It turned out real nice. Don't say that."

Her mother-in-law laughed. "They used to call garden buildings, like that one, follies back a long time ago. But they were a little different than the beautiful gazebo that Garrett designed."

Mama drew closer, with the girls following behind. "The only folly I know is Theo thinking my daughter was runnin' a tea shop."

"And your daughter, allowing him to think so!" Mrs. Reynold's sharp retort caused the silk flowers on the crown of her cream-colored hat to shake.

Theo raised his hands. "See here. All is well now."

Both mothers nodded. And Lilly had to agree.

The End

Author's Notes

I was surprised at how early the Soo Locks construction was begun, when I began researching this book. I had no idea they were working on the original Locks near the time of the Civil War! Growing up in the Upper Peninsula and having attended Lake Superior State College (now University) I was very familiar with the modern-day locks. It was fun imagining the early locks, which my character Theo is helping to modernize.

The 1890's were full of inventions. Theo uses Lifebuoy soap, an 1895 creation from England, in this story. The soap was purported to have medicinal properties. During this time period, lots of quackery and snake oil salesman was going on. I included that aspect when I had Theo's and Lilly's mothers talked about Mrs. Smith's "cure" which was really God restoring her hope.

The street names in the story are real. For instance, Theo's boardinghouse is on Bingham. Businesses in the story are on Ashmun, which they are in modern-day Sault Ste. Marie. The Soo Locks are on Water Street. Portage, which is where Lilly's "not-a-tea-shop!" is! Portage rounds a curve and I picture Lilly's house near the curve. One feature on the 1895 map, which is no longer there, was Fort Brady. Apparently there was some resistance from the army when the Locks were to be built. As can be seen, the Corps of Engineers has their Locks and there is no army fort on Water Street any longer. However, you will find Coast Guard a little further down. The amount of ships, in particular the distinctive iron ore freighters, going through the Locks in astounding. I highly recommend that if you visit the Locks that you also take a boat tour through them. You'll find the transitioning from one level of water to the other, with the Locks, to be quite amazing.

Sault Ste. Marie has a fascinating history. I remember, as a child, celebrating the 300th anniversary of the city. There is tremendous Native American history here, especially the Chippewa tribe, and of course the French and fur traders. Across the St. Mary's River is the twin city of Sault Ste. Marie, Ontario, Canada. The Canadians also have a Lock built about the same time as my hero was helping get the American Lock built.

Inspiration for the hoarder of high quality teacups and teapots came from an outing in Virginia with blogger friend, Anne Payne. We stumbled upon a bed and breakfast that had every nook and cranny filled with antiques, mostly teasets and china. When I turned over one of the cups and saw the maker's mark I was shocked! Here were all these rare antique teacups and saucers right out in plain view as if they were for sale. But they weren't! They were part of the décor! So the notion of a hoarder aunt whose house was misconstrued as a shop was born. And now you've read Lilly's story – thanks!

For those of you who enjoyed The Christy Lumber Camp Series, this novella includes one of my favorite characters -- Garrett, AKA "Moose" who is a married man with a family in this story! I envision Lilly's novella becoming part of a "Christy Cousins" trilogy. Maybe one of those floral-named sisters will get her own romance, too!

Acknowledgements

Thank you Father God, for enabling me to write this story, for Your glory! God bless my family for supporting my story writing, too!

Much thanks to Beta readers: Cheryl Baranski, Regina Fujitani, Andrea Byers, Sydney Anderson, and Tina Rice and to Advance reader: Joy Gibson. My Pagels Pals team members are wonderful! Thanks for all the help with suggestions for names and your ongoing prayer for me and my writing! Thanks, Anne Payne, for coming with me on my research outing for colonial era which instead morphed into this turn-of-the-century novella!

Thank you to Susan James, Librarian, Sault Ste. Marie, Michigan, for the 1895 map of the Soo, which was very helpful.

Thanks 1k1hr Facebook group and to Ruth Logan Herne, who is always there as an inspiration. Thank you to Melanie, Sarah, and Julie – just knowing you are there if I need you is a comfort. Thank you to the Overcoming with God blogger team, Diana, Teresa, Noela, and Bonnie for being an ongoing support!

Thank you, Roseanna White, for the beautiful new cover!

About the Author & Social Media

Carrie Fancett Pagels, Ph.D., is a multi-published award-winning author of Christian historical romance. Twenty-five years as a psychologist didn't "cure" her overactive imagination! She resides with her family in the Historic Triangle of Virginia, which is perfect for her love of history. Carrie loves to read, bake, bead, and travel – but not all at the same time!

Sign up for Carrie's newsletter and keep in touch as well as win prizes and get the inside scoop on her activities – email her at cfpagels@gmail.com to sign up.

Website: www.carriefancettpagels.com
Blogs: www.OvercomingWithGod.com
and www.ColonialQuills.org
Active on Facebook, Twitter (cfpagels), Pinterest, goodreads, and LinkedIn.

Other Stories from Carrie Fancett Pagels

<u>2017</u>

"Love's Escape" – a novella in *The Captive Brides Collection* (Barbour, November, 2017)

My Heart Belongs on Mackinac Island, a novel (Barbour, July 2017).

"Dime Novel Suitor" - a novella in *Seven Brides for Seven Mail-Order Grooms* (Barbour, June, 2017).

Tea Shop Folly, 2nd edition, Book One in The Christy Cousins' Series, novella re-released under new cover (Hearts Overcoming Press, March, 2017).

<u>2016</u>

"Requilted With Love" - a novella in *The Blue Ribbon Brides Collection* (Barbour Publishing, November 2016).

Saving the Marquise's Granddaughter, a novel (White Rose/Pelican Book Group, June 2016).

The Steeplechase - a novella (Forget Me Not Romances, February 2016).

Return to Shirley Plantation: A Civil War Romance, 2nd edition, novella re-released under new cover (Hearts Overcoming Press, January, 2016).

<u>2015</u>

The Substitute Bride - novella (Hearts Overcoming Press, October, 2015). **Maggie Award finalist** 2016 in Romance Novellas.

Lilacs for Juliana, a novel (Hearts Overcoming Press, August, 2015) Book Three in The Christy Lumber Camp Series.

The Lumberjack's Ball, a novel (Hearts Overcoming Press, April, 2015). Book Two in The Christy Lumber Camp Series

2014

The Fruitcake Challenge (Hearts Overcoming Press, September 2014). Selah Award Finalist and Family Fiction Book of the Year finalist. Part of The Christmas Traditions Collection and also Book One in The Christy Lumber Camp Series.

"The Quilting Contest," short story award winner in historical category, published in *"The Story 2014" Anthology* (Family Fiction, 2014.)

2013

"Snowed In," in *A Cup of Christmas Cheer* (Guideposts Books, October, 2013) a two-volume hardcover set.

THANK YOU FOR READING THIS NOVELLA!

If you enjoyed this novella, an honest review is always appreciated!